BLACK SUN Nº.2

SIX-GUN SHUFFLE

by

David Dixon

SIX-GUN SHUFFLE

First Edition Copyright © 2021 by Dark Brew Press

All rights reserved. No part of this publication may be reproduced, distributed, or transmitted in any form or by any means, including photocopying, recording, or other electronic or mechanical methods, without the prior written permission of the publisher, except in the case of brief quotations embodied in critical reviews and certain other non-commercial uses permitted by copyright law.

This is a work of fiction. Any characters, names, places, or likenesses are purely fictional. Resemblances to any of the items listed above are merely coincidental.

For permission requests, please contact the publisher, Dark Brew Press, via e-mail, with subject "Attention: Permissions Coordinator," at: editor@darkbrewpress.com

ISBN
Paperback: 978-1-990317-05-7
eBook: 978-1-990317-04-0

Interior design by Crystal L. Kirkham
www.darkbrewpress.com

<u>THE BLACK SUN SERIES</u>
by David Dixon

The Damsel

Six-Gun Shuffle

Hell Hath No Fury
(*Coming Soon*)

CHAPTER ONE

You ever noticed how something can seem small and insignificant when it starts and then—boom—the next thing you know that little speck of light behind you is a missile screaming right for your ass? Life is like that a lot for me and the boss, it seems. One minute something is a minor inconvenience and the next minute it's a matter of life and death.

The boss and I were at Holloway spaceport on Yaeger VII, having just completed a run from Piker's Distillery on Talos. We'd gotten confirmation that our payment had come through, so we trudged across the icy, windblown spaceport toward our beat-up Black Sun 490

I took a worried glance at the sky. Overhead, massive black clouds churned like my stomach after too many White Russians. The locals had warned us that the storm that was coming would snow the whole city in for two or three days, if not more. While ordinarily I wouldn't have minded a break from the confines the ship for a bit, Yaeger VII was hardly the place to do it. The only thing Yaeger VII was known for was a few second-rate casinos, shitty weather, bad beer, and obnoxious locals. Kinda reminded me of New New England. I scowled and fished a cigarette out of my shirt pocket.

The boss watched me light it and gave me that grin he has when he thinks he's about to be clever. "Man, Snake, you sure are smoking a lot these days."

I snorted. "I've always smoked."

"Yeah, but it seems like it's more here of late. When we left Greenly, you smoked like a chimney until we ran into Carla on Tayir. And you practically quit while we were on Rucker Watson's with her, and as soon as we left you started back up again. I think they're like your replacement for Carla."

I took a drag before I answered. "At least I've got someone to replace."

His grin disappeared.

I clapped him on the back. "Better luck next time, champ."

"Have I ever mentioned how much I hate you?" the boss replied.

I shrugged. "Maybe, but I probably wasn't listening."

"Hey, Snake, there's a pair of guys hanging out beside the ship," the boss said, suddenly serious. He nodded to the starboard side of the ship a hundred meters away, where a pair of men stood in the shadow of our Black Sun 490 looking up at the sky. My gut tightened. They were probably just using it as shelter against the wind, but in our line of work, you could never be too careful.

As we drew closer, the boss tucked his hands under his arms, which to someone else might make it seem like he was just keeping them warm, but I knew he had his right hand on the grip of the .45 revolver tucked in his shoulder holster.

A loud roar passing overhead made me flinch, and I looked up to see a large, ducted hovercraft coming in low. The pilot flared the engines, which sent freezing wind and stinging pellets of ice flying. He landed too close to our ship, and as the boss and I stared in outrage, the side door dropped open and half a dozen more men stepped out, trotting out onto the spaceport tarmac like they owned the place. One of them actually leaned up against our Black Sun 490, a move that in the spacer world is the sort of etiquette violation that would normally earn you anywhere from a broken nose to a bullet in the brainpan, depending on how far out in the Fringe you are.

The boss and I stomped toward the ship. My blood was boiling. What kind of asshole could possibly think he had the right to just walk up to our shit and lean on it like he was the goddamned UNF General Secretary or something? Did these clowns have a death wish?

"Yo, dipshit," the boss shouted across the frozen spaceport. "Touch my ship again and see what happens."

The man who'd leaned against it leapt away like he'd been shocked. By now we were close enough to see that they were dressed in the sort of expensive cold weather gear meant to go ice climbing on Titan or something but usually used to keep super rich pricks from suffering even the smallest amount of dick shrinkage.

"Excuse me?" one of the men snapped. "Are you talking to us? Who the fuck do you think you are? Who gave you permission to be here?"

"The fuck you say?" the boss growled as we drew closer. "'Who gave you permission?' is the question,' because last time I checked, I didn't give you permission to touch shit."

"We're here for the video shoot and we rented the whole spaceport," the man huffed. "Everything here is supposed to be available for use."

"Well, you've been misinformed," I answered. "This is our ship, and it's not available for whatever the fuck you think it is. So, you got like maybe five seconds to clear out before things get ugly."

"I think there's been some sort of misunderstanding," he replied.

"Five," I said as I took another menacing step closer to the ship. I'd been in the game long enough to know that these were the type who'd never even match the ante, much less stick around for the call.

"But I—"

"Four," the boss said, slapping his fist into his palm.

"Can't we just—"

"Three," I said, sighing as I flicked my cigarette away.

The men scampered toward the hovercraft. The boss and I dropped the cargo ramp and strolled inside, chuckling.

Fucking earthworms—the same on every planet.

We got to work doing maintenance, as always. I worked inside, topping off fluid levels, replacing scrubber filters in the life support system, and recalibrating my turret servos. The boss worked outside, running down an intermittent fault in the J7 junction box that kept shorting out our gravimetric sensor every time the shield generator cycled.

He walked back up the cargo ramp ten minutes later, soaked in sweat and without his coat, muttering curses under his breath. I looked up from the left-side scrubber bank. "What's up?" I asked.

"Fucking J7 cover is stuck."

"Yeah. It was that same way the last time I worked on it. I think the locking ring is busted. You're probably going to have to pry it off, and that'll mean we—"

One of the men from earlier appeared just at the base of the ramp, careful not to actually set foot on it. He cleared his throat.

The boss turned to face him, but before either one of us could tell the guy to get lost, another man joined him, and my gut tightened. The second guy was no rich asshole—redundant, I know—in five thousand credits' worth of winter gear. He was a hulking bruiser in black boots, jeans, and only a long-sleeved T-shirt despite the fact that the first few snowflakes had already begun to fall. This was the type of guy who wouldn't just see the ante, but might even raise it.

"See, Liz," the man from earlier said to his new friend, "these are the two I was talking about."

Liz looked up the ramp at us, and I got the feeling he was sizing us up. I took a drag from my cigarette and tried to be nonchalant. In this business, sometimes it's best just to let people sort out for themselves who they're dealing with.

"You giving my man a hard time?" Liz finally said.

The boss shrugged. "Not really. But if your man comes over here touching our shit again, he might get one."

Liz nodded. "I get you, but here's the thing: you're not supposed to be here."

My expression didn't change, but something about the way Liz spoke set little warning alarms chiming in my head. He had the sort of quiet, steely confidence that only came from having done this before—and coming out on top.

"I got a paid invoice for three hundred credits for the use of this pad and utilities that says otherwise," the boss said.

Liz shook his head. "I don't care if you got a paid invoice for fucking Mars. We paid for the whole spaceport. For a video shoot."

Liz casually slid up his left sleeve to reveal a brilliant red lizard tattoo, and suddenly the reason for the "Liz" nickname clicked into place—Liz for "lizard." Half a second later, something else clicked into place for me. That tattoo, like the snake coiled around my left arm, wasn't just there for decoration. It was a gang sign, which in this case meant he either had been or still was a member of the Iguanas, a sector gang that ran Z on the regular and occasionally pulled side gigs as "personal protection."

Fuck.

Beside me, the boss flared his nostrils. "But like I said, we already paid for the pad, and I'm not paying for another. We got maintenance to do. But you let us finish up our shit here, and we'll be glad to get gone. We weren't planning on sticking around anyway."

Liz flicked his eyes to the man who'd told us to move the first time. With Liz by his side, he'd regained some of his earlier rich asshole confidence. He shook his head. "No way, Liz. We're behind a day already, and camera and crew time is running the company four grand a minute. Michael is already unhappy with how things are going, and I need him in a good mood for the video. I want them gone."

Liz looked back at us. "You heard him."

"We already paid for the pad," the boss protested. "Call station control. They can't just—"

Liz chuckled wickedly. "Go ahead. Call 'em."

Holloway Center Control, of course, sided with Liz, giving us some story about how buried deep in the standard twenty-page rental contract was some bullshit clause about "terms and conditions subject to change without notice."

"So, there you go," Liz said after our ten-minute argument with Holloway Center Control. "Get lost."

"And if I say no?" the boss asked, his hand resting on his pistol.

"I'll call station security out here and they can move you, if you want to go the hard way," Liz said with a shrug. "They're good friends of mine, but they're not very careful people. Something would probably get broken, and I don't think you want that."

The boss and I exchanged a glance, and I hoped he could read in my look that this was a fight we probably wouldn't win. I don't mind dragging things out as a matter of principle, but I also don't like doing any more maintenance than I have to— on the ship or my face.

"You know what? Fuck this," the man with Liz said. "We're wasting time and if the weather gets too bad, I'm going to have to delay the shoot again. Let them stay, for all I care. I'll edit their piece-of-shit rust bucket out in post." He looked at us and narrowed his eyes. "Just close the cargo bay, and you can have your precious pad back when we finish. But you have got to stay inside. If one of you comes out and fucks up my shot, I'm going to have station security move your ship and I'll sue you for every fucking credit you've got, you hear me?"

The boss's jaw worked, but he nodded. "We'll stay inside, but don't touch anything out there, you got it? This ship may be a 'piece-of-shit rust bucket,' but it's my piece-of-shit rust bucket."

I decided now was not the time to point out that technically, the ship was half mine, too.

"Sure, whatever," the man said with a dismissive wave, and he and Liz disappeared back out onto the tarmac.

———————————

Five hours later, it was almost dark and we were almost crazy. It turns out the video shoot was for a music holo, and whatever song they were shooting for either only had four words—*baby, baby, baby, baby*—repeated over and over again, or they shot the same goddamn scene a hundred times. Either way, by the time they were done, if I heard one more *baby*, I was going to put a pistol in my mouth.

As soon as their hovercraft took off, passing overhead and shaking the ship, the boss and I went outside to stretch our legs. The air was cold like a knife between the ribs, and it was all I could do to smoke without feeling like my fingers were going to freeze off.

The boss clapped his bare arms around himself for warmth and disappeared around the front of the ship, only to return a moment later, glancing across the empty docking pads.

"Where's my coat?" he asked.

"The black one? How the fuck should I know? I'm not your mom, man."

"I left it out front, on top of the toolbox next to the J7 box."

"Maybe it blew across the—"

"No. I looped it through the handle. Plus, it'd be blowing around out here if the wind got it."

I shivered against the cold. "I dunno, boss. If you left it there, it should still be there."

A sudden look of fury crossed his face. "I'll bet one of that piece-of-shit film crew took it! I told him not to touch our stuff. If I see somebody wearing it, I'm going to break their goddamn arms."

I snorted. "Dude. Why would somebody steal your nasty-ass old coat?" I asked. "But whatever, it doesn't matter. I think we got another—"

"I don't want another coat, damn it! I want mine. And I wanna know who took it."

I gave him an incredulous look. "It's just a coat, man. If you want another one, I know we're hard up for cash, but I think we can afford a coat. It isn't like that thing was the height of fashion anyway."

He stomped up the ramp. "That coat has sentimental value."

"Sentimental value?" I asked, following him. "You shitting me right now?"

"No, I'm serious. When I got this ship, only two things came with it." He pointed to the .45 revolver hanging in its shoulder rig by the hatch to the crew compartment. "The first was that pistol. The second was the coat. Now they're my pistol and my coat. And I want my damn coat."

"You're wrong. Three things came with the ship. That pistol, that coat, and a fuckton of headaches," I cracked.

"Goddamnit, Snake, I'm serious. I want my fucking coat back."

"Well, I got no idea where it went, all right? But if I see it, I'll make sure to tell it to come home and that daddy misses it very much."

I chuckled at his scowl.

"Look," the boss said. "I get that you can't get it right now, because your tiny little reptile brain is incapable of understanding how somebody else might feel, but let me put it in terms you can understand. How long have you had that ratty green duffel bag you always carry around with you?"

"I dunno, as long as I can remember. At least since I was ten or twelve, 'cause whenever me and my mom got kicked out of a place, that's what I put all my stuff in when we left."

"Okay, fine. So, say somebody stole your duffel bag, what—"

"Nobody's gonna steal my duffel bag," I objected.

"Jesus, Snake! Work with me. Say somebody did steal it, because—somehow—they were even worse off than you. If somebody sketched that bag from you, what would you do?"

I gave it a moment's thought before I answered. "I'd fuck 'em right up."

"Right. Same thing with my coat."

"Whatever, bossman. If we're out and about and you see somebody with your coat on, I guess I'll give you a hand, if it means that much to you." I shook my head and went back to working on the voltage calculations I'd abandoned earlier, figuring I'd was the last I'd ever hear about his stupid coat.

I was wrong, of course.

CHAPTER TWO

That night, Holloway Center Control fucked us over for a second time by informing us that the weather was going to close the spaceport for at least three more days. After that news, the boss and I went to grab a bite to eat at a ratty American-themed bar at the far edge of Holloway's nightlife district. As we sat drinking bad beer and eating greasy fries, he was still complaining about the loss of his stupid coat.

"I swear to god, Snake, I'm gonna find out where those assholes are staying and I'm gonna kick in every damn door in that hotel until I find my coat," he said before polishing off another glass of beer.

"Uh-huh," I answered absently, leaning back in the booth to try to catch a weather forecast displayed on one of the bar's holoscreens. The forecast showed a huge front moving through and predicted high winds and almost a meter of snow accumulation before the bartender changed the channel.

The weather disappeared, replaced onscreen by footage I recognized had been shot at the spaceport all afternoon, with the headline *Pop Superstar Films New Video at Holloway Station*! I muttered a curse under my breath for the production having stranded us on Yaeger, then the holo cut to a young man in his early twenties wearing what I guessed were supposed to be the clothes of a space pirate, as imagined by someone who'd never actually met one. His whole vibe screamed "rich-kid chic": expensive tattoos; an entitled, pouty look that called out for a facial rearrangement courtesy of somebody's fist; slick, stylish hair; and topped off with an easy smile that made girls swoon. Just as I was about to look away, a different shot of him cutting through a crowd to get into a nightclub caught my eye.

Draped across his faux-pirate shoulders was a faded black duster.

"Yo, bossman," I said without taking my eyes off the screen. "Check out the holo. Is that your coat?"

He watched for a second, then slammed his empty glass to the table. "That motherfucker. C'mon, let's go get it back."

"Dude, they're not gonna let us anywhere near the door to that club. Not a chance in hell we'd get in anyway, much less when they've got some rich asshole there partying."

"I don't care. I'm getting in, and I'm getting my coat. Come on." The boss stood, left a few bills on the table, and went to the bar to ask about the club in the holo.

I sighed and gulped down the last of my beer, figuring this was going to be one of those nights that ended with us beaten up by bouncers, in police custody, or both.

So, all in all, a pretty normal planetside night for us.

The bartender told us the club was a downtown joint named Club Seventy-Two, and a fifteen-minute cab ride later, the boss and I found ourselves in a long line outside.

"See? I told you," I said to him over the buzz of the crowd. "This place is gonna be packed, and there's no way some lowlifes like us are getting in. Not tonight. Not with him here."

"I'm not leaving without my coat."

"Fine, fine," I muttered, and tucked my hands under my arms to keep them warm.

We'd waited in line for a few more minutes before the boss gave me a nudge in the ribs. "Snake, check out the blonde. Up front, by the club entrance. I think she's checking us out, man." I followed his line of sight between a pair of bouncers to a gorgeous twenty-something blonde poured into a shimmery gold dress that looked way too cold for the weather. As an apparent nod to the filming and famous guest, she'd finished her ensemble off with an obviously fake gun belt and pistol. She didn't look in our direction.

I rolled my eyes. "The 'blonde'? You mean the club hostess? Somehow, I doubt she's checking us out, bro. She's probably looking for her boyfriend out here with the rest of the pricks. Also, if she's checking us out, you know she's really checking me out."

"Har har. No, I haven't managed to forget that, thanks," he grumbled. "But how about you put your charm shit to good use and go up there and get her to let us in? You can tell she's the one calling the shots out here. Look at the way she talks to the bouncers."

"I dunno, man," I said. "I know this is a foreign concept to you, but there's a certain art to this, and just walking up and saying 'Hey girl, I know everybody and their fuckin' brother has hit on you tonight, but how about you get us into the club because you accidentally looked at my boy and now, he thinks you're falling for him' is not gonna work. No use talking to her, trust me."

"I don't fucking believe it. I never thought I'd see the day, but it's finally happened," the boss said, wonder in his voice. "My god, she actually did it."

"Huh?"

"Carla. Carla flat out broke you, didn't she? Ever since Greenly, your game has been shit. Every bar or club we go to, you hang out for an hour before you're like 'this place is crap, these girls are lame, blah blah blah,' and then you head back to the ship or the hotel and sit around and drink by yourself. She's got you. You're whipped."

"That's bullshit," I scoffed. "I'm fine. It's just that I keep hanging out with your lame ass, so we keep going to lame-ass places."

The boss's eyes gleamed. "Oh no, Snake, I know you well enough to know when you're full of shit — which is most of the time, by the way. But you're straight lying. She's got you good, man."

"Like I said, boss. Bullshit. Carla hasn't done shit to my game. I still got it."

"Okay then, if you still got it, go prove it. Go talk to her and get us in. Then I promise I won't make your pining-for-Carla ass stay in there any longer than it takes for me to get my coat back."

"Fine. Look and learn," I snapped. "These circumstances are hardly ideal, but I'll get it done. You just sit back here and take notes while I get us in so we can get your stupid jacket."

I gritted my teeth and made my way through the crowd. The truth was, the boss was right about one thing: ever since Carla and I had gotten together, I'd been unsuccessful with any other girls. But it wasn't because Carla had some sort of special hold on me, right?

Right?

I squeezed past two guys in suits waiting to get in and tried to get the attractive blonde's attention.

"Hey! Hey, what's—" I started.

"Get lost."

I winced. This wasn't going to be easy. "Aww, come on, why—"

"Get. Fucking. Gone." She crossed her arms in front of her and refused to even make eye contact.

I wondered if the boss was right. I wasn't used to getting rejected before I'd even gotten a single sentence out of my mouth. Time for a change of tactics.

"We're part of the dance crew," I said. "Look at us, we're in costume and—"

"Bullshit," she said. "You two are actual space scum, not the pretend type."

"Oh yeah," I asked. "And how do you know that?"

"You're both way too old to be dancers. And your friend's too ugly."

An opening. I smiled. "Well, you got us there. And, by the way, I'd love to hear you tell him that."

"I'm not talking to you anymore."

"Awww. Let's see... My friend's enlisting tomorrow and—nah, he's too old for that one, isn't he? How about 'my friend is dying of cancer and this might be his last night out.' You heard that one?"

Despite trying to hide it, a smile flashed across her face before she could stop it.

"Aha!" I said. "So, you have heard that one. Damn. Well, I guess I'll have to go with the truth."

"Oh my god," she deadpanned. "Has it come to that?"

"Eh. We'll see. If it doesn't work, I'll come up with something else."

"She already said get lost," one of the bouncers cut in. "So get lost."

I shrugged. "Fine," I told the bouncer. "But she'll never find out what the real reason we want in is, and I guarantee she hasn't heard this one." I turned to walk away.

The blonde's voice stopped me. "Wait. Let's hear it."

I turned back around, grin on my face. "You gonna let me in?"

She feigned disinterest, but there was a flicker in her eyes. "No promises, but go ahead. Tell me."

"That guy is my boss, and believe it or not, whoever the big-time singer kid is in there stole his fucking coat. And he wants it back."

She laughed—a sweet sort of laugh that normally would have sent me into close-the-deal mode, but for some reason, tonight didn't seem the night. A very tiny part of me wondered whether the boss was more right about Carla's effect on me than I'd thought.

"Whoa," she said. "First off, that 'big-time singer kid' you're talking about is Michael Ver— only like one of the biggest music stars in the world right now. Sold-out concerts from Mars to Paris V. You know, that Michael Ver—the one with all the fans? The 'LoVers,' they call them? And you say you've never heard of him?"

I shook my head. "Nope."

"That's insane."

"It is what it is."

"Okay, so I believe you two space jockeys spend too much time out there in the black to know what's up, but you said your friend is after his coat?" she asked. "For real?"

"For real. Somebody sketched it off our ship while they were filming, and next thing we know, dipshit's wearing it on TV."

"He could just buy a new coat, you know," she pointed out.

"Yeah. That's what I said. But the coat has 'sentimental value' according to him."

"That's about the dumbest thing I've heard all night, but at least it's original," she said. "You two can come in. I do have to say this officially, though—don't cause too much of a mess, please."

I nodded. "Of course. And, uh, unofficially?"

"Ver and his crew are a bunch of assholes that treat everybody else like shit." She smiled.

"Sorry to hear that. But we'll be good," I lied.

She laughed. "Famous last words."

"Yep."

I waved to the boss and he cut his way through the crowd, as the better dressed, richer set murmured their complaints. He ignored them and the bouncers as well, although he did cast more than one glance at the hostess.

"Give it up," I whispered to him. "It ain't gonna happen."

He shook his head but didn't answer as the hostess pushed the club door open. The place was packed with sweaty rich kids, the bass line thumped loud enough to make my heart beat in time, and the house lighting flickered fast enough to cause a seizure.

I hate those kinds of clubs.

Just before she let the door close behind us, she whispered something in my boss's ear. He scowled.

"Yo, what'd she say?" I yelled over the club's pulsing techno beat.

He mumbled something, but I couldn't make it out.

"What?" I asked again.

He leaned close and shouted. "She said to tell you her shift ends at one, you sonofabitch!"

I laughed. "Let's find your coat, then. Maybe she'll have a friend for you."

Whatever he said in response got lost in the music, but I figured it was probably an insult, so I didn't bother asking him to repeat it.

I scanned the club, looking for signs of our duster-stealing pop star. It took me longer than it should have because of the music, the mass of writhing bodies on the dance floor, and the strobe lighting, but I finally caught a glimpse of him across the club in a dimly lit corner of expansive booths I figured was the VIP section, surrounded by the usual constellation of hot girls and rich douches that orbit most stars. I elbowed the boss in the ribs and pointed across the club. He nodded and pointed to the bar. Puzzled, I followed him to the monstrosity of glass, neon, mirrors, and—somewhere, I assumed—alcohol.

A brief, merciful pause in the techno-racket they called music allowed conversation at below ear-splitting level.

"What's up, boss? I thought you wanted to get your coat back?" I asked.

He shrugged. "I will. I just figured we oughta get a drink first, since I got a feeling we're about to get kicked outta here for fucking with the guest of honor."

"Works for me."

He opened a tab I figured we'd not stick around to close, then ordered an expensive scotch while I got a bourbon double. We sipped our drinks as we turned our attention back across the club to Michael Ver, who seemed to be telling a story, judging by the rapt attention of his flunkie audience.

"So, what's the plan?" I asked the boss.

"I'm gonna walk up and tell him to give me back my coat."

I could think of a whole host of reasons why it wasn't going to be that simple, but I chose the most obvious. "And if he doesn't want to?"

"I drop his ass," he said, pounding his right fist into his left palm.

"Uh-huh. Okay, well, how exactly do you think you're gonna get that close to him? Remember his boy 'Liz'? He's gonna be there too, I bet."

The boss didn't answer. Instead, he unzipped the gray fleece I'd loaned him as a replacement for his duster. I saw his T-shirt underneath—and his shoulder holster.

Jesus.

I'd brought my knife like I always did, but I'd never heard a single story that began "So this one time this guy pulled a pistol in the club and..." that didn't end in tragedy. I started thinking maybe my boss had gone just a little overboard.

"Whoa, man. I'm down for getting roughed up, arrested, fined—whatever, you know? I mean, that's just the business. But I think, uh, going all Murderfest 3000 up in here might not be the best idea. It's a coat, remember?"

"I'm not gonna shoot anybody, Snake. This is just to let 'em know I'm serious. They'll back the fuck off. Look around. Everybody else in here is just pretending to be us. We are us." He gestured to the club.

I took another look around and noticed that indeed there were a lot of people dressed almost exactly like us, except there was some undefinable... something that just wasn't quite right. If I had to guess, it was probably that their faded gray T-shirts were brand new and probably cost four hundred credits apiece, while mine were four or five years old and I'd gotten them off a street vendor in Youzan for half a credit a pop, and that their jeans cost more than every stitch of clothing I'd ever owned.

"I know what you mean, but still... A lot of these guys are inner-system-off-world posers, sure, but not everybody is. Yaeger's got some real tough guys," I warned.

"Eh. Maybe so, but they're all at real bars, not dance clubs like this place."

"Let's hope so," I muttered as I followed him across the dance floor over to the VIP area.

A pair of rich guys in their twenties wearing the same faux-pirate-style getup as our target seemed to serve as the unofficial gatekeepers. They eyed us with disdain as we approached.

"No visitors. He's not signing autographs tonight," one of them told us.

"Do we look like we want an autograph?" the boss said. "We're here to see him about something he owes us."

"He said 'no visitors,'" the other one answered.

"It's not that we didn't hear him," I said. "It's that we don't give a fuck. Move it." I took a step toward them. One of them startled backward, but the other hesitated, then held his ground.

The boss opened his jacket, revealing his pistol. "This one is real, okay? So, let's be smart about this, aight?"

The two scampered off in opposite directions and we stepped into Michael Ver's inner circle.

The same handsome, smug-looking prick I'd seen on the holo looked up when we parted his crowd of adoring girls, my boss's black duster draped across his shoulders like a cape. His eyes flashed with annoyance, and he nodded almost imperceptibly at someone in the shadows to his left. In the dark, a big figure moved toward us, and I figured if my boss planned to take Ver himself, that meant Liz was my responsibility.

I met the goon before he could reach the boss, E-14 combat knife in my right hand and held a few centimeters from Liz's stomach. He looked down, then back at me with a scowl.

"Listen," I said in a low voice. "Nobody needs to get hurt here, least of all you. My boy just wants his coat back from your boy. No need to get jumpy. You don't seem the hero type, and neither am I, which in your case means just chill, and in my case means I absolutely won't hesitate to open you right up if you try to fuck with us, got it?"

I admit, I laid it on a bit thick, but when you're doing this sort of thing it's better somebody thinks you're too serious than not serious enough. Liz didn't answer, but there was an unexpected gleam in his eyes—if I hadn't known better, I would have thought he seemed almost pleased. He shrugged and slouched into the nearest chair.

Michael Ver gave a pouty sneer and leaned back in the booth, as if he were the king of the fucking world.

"What the fuck are you doing? Do you know who I am?" he asked the boss.

"I really don't, actually. And I don't care. All I know is you're wearing my coat."

"Finders keepers, bro," Ver answered.

"That's cute," the boss sneered. "It'll look nice on your tombstone. Now, give me back my damn coat."

A few of the girls tittered as Ver stood up and shrugged the coat off his shoulders. Under the duster he wore a white wifebeater that showed off his sculpted, tattooed arms. He made a show of flexing his chest for a second, then for some reason, he pulled off the wifebeater to reveal chiseled six-pack abs, even more trendy tattoos, and a pair of platinum chains.

"No." Ver brushed his hair out of his face before narrowing his eyes at the boss in some sort of holo-imitation of what I guess he thought was a tough guy. "And you and your friend got about five seconds to get out of here before I kick both your asses."

I snorted. He may have thought his chiseled physique translated into fighting prowess, but I knew better. My partner had a few extra pounds of flab on him, sure, but he'd been in more fights than Ver had had hot meals. I'd met a hundred young wannabe toughs like Ver in my time, and ninety-nine percent of them had started crying the first time they tasted their own blood. I had a feeling Ver was going to end his night in tears.

"And you're next," Ver said, pointing a tattooed finger at me.

"There's not going to be a next, trust me," my partner warned the pop star. "Just give me back my coat so I don't have to kick your ass in front of all your friends. Gonna be hard to finish your video when you look like you fell down a flight of stairs."

The kid gave another pandering smile to the crowd, then made a quick move toward the boss. I think Ver must have thought he was going to make my boss flinch, but he didn't understand that in our line of work, when somebody asks you to tango, it's impolite not to dance to the tune.

The boss hit Ver with a left jab, right in the nose.

The punch must have been the first time anybody had actually stepped to him, because instead of getting his guard up, Ver started to protest.

"Hey, you—" was all he managed to whine before the boss's right hook caught him in the side of the jaw and sent him to the ground like a sack of wet shit.

I winced. The boss and I had gotten into an actual knock-down-drag-out in our first year of flying together in deep space off Al-Hatar—over what, I can't remember—and I'd been on the receiving end of one of those hooks. It had not been pleasant.

Ver's admirers screamed and gasped and shouted for security, but nobody made a move toward us. The boss gave Ver a solid kick in the ribs before he scooped up his duster and finished Ver's drink from off the table just as the club lights flickered on.

For his part, Michael Ver stayed down, moaning.

"Well, looks like it's time for us to head out," I told Liz with a grin. He still hadn't moved from his chair. Some security he was. "Tell your boy to stay away from our stuff, unless he wants to get straight wrecked again."

Liz's eyes flicked down to his pop-star boss on the floor, then back to me, but he didn't answer as the boss and I made our way through the crowd to leave.

We ducked out a fire exit before the bouncers ever reached the table, then down the alley and onto another side street. I lit a cigarette in the falling snow, and the boss put his black duster on with a smile.

"So, what was he drinking anyway?" I asked.

"Hell, if I know," the boss said. "Tasted like some sort of fruity liqueur and champagne, I think."

"Fuckin' figures."

"Yep."

CHAPTER THREE

We made our way down the snowy side street to another bar, the kind without a line full of pretentious assholes in expensive suits and pretend tough guys. By the time we took our barstools, a holo-screen in the corner already showed shaky video of my partner's encounter with Ver, filmed on someone's phone or ocular implants. The bartender glanced at us, did a double take, and then looked back up at the screen.

"Is that you?" he asked the boss, pointing up to where the screen showed him punching Michael Ver in slow motion.

"Could be me, yeah," the boss said with a grin.

The bartender beamed. "Whatcha want? It's on the house. I hate that dude. My girlfriend loves his stupid ass."

"Scotch. Double."

"Done."

The boss chuckled and turned to me with a self-satisfied smile. "Dude, this is gonna be awesome. I—"

A young guy who was obviously well into his night of drinking interrupted us, his words slurred. "Yo, man, you look just like that guy on the holos, punching Michael Ver—'zat you?"

The boss shrugged. "Yeah."

"Holy shit, bro! You're my hero. Fuckin' A, dude. That asshole is ruining music." He waved over a passing server and pointed at my partner.

"Scott, man, check it out. This—this guy—here's the dude that fucked up Michael Ver. Hook him up with a drink, would ya?"

The server broke out into a wide smile and called out to the rest of the bar. "Hey, everybody listen up! We got ourselves a bona fide hero here tonight. Sitting up here is the man who knocked Michael Ver the fuck out!"

Most of the men in the place hooted, but several of the ladies shook their heads in disgust while a few others seemed almost teary. I chuckled. It looked like most of the guys shared my opinion of Ver's music, but I had to hand it to "Ver"—he seemed to have it going on with the women. Another round of drinks arrived in front of us, followed by another, and then another. We'd drunk enough to get to feeling pretty good when the boss turned to me to announce his intention of parlaying his newfound fame into some luck with the ladies.

"Everybody in this place loves me, man. And I'm not gonna let it go to waste. I'm gonna go talk to her," he said with a nod to a gorgeous girl whose dark skin contrasted with her skintight red jeans and yellow silk top. She looked our way for an instant before returning to her conversation with her attractive blonde friend.

"So, we've reached this part of the night, huh?" I made a show of checking the clock behind the bar. "A bit early, don't you think?"

"What do you mean? What 'part of the night' is that?"

"The part that ends with you giving some girl sad puppy dog eyes as she gets into a cab without you."

He scowled. "Oh, you got jokes, huh? Well, you wait and see. Tonight is going to go good for me. I can feel it."

"Nope. What you can feel is all that booze. I'm telling you, that girl isn't gonna have a thing to do with you, but if you want me to, I'll go over there with you and help break the ice and—"

"No. Abso-fucking-lutely not. Every time you talk to a girl I'm interested in, you wind up sleeping with her, and—you know what? Don't even look at her, okay? Just... look over there or something." He pointed to the opposite wall.

I chuckled as I lit a cigarette. "And that is exactly why you should listen to me. Clearly, I know more about women than you do. Doesn't matter. I'm tired and I'm headed over to a place downtown I saw advertised on TV anyway. Give it your best shot, but don't try to bullshit me tomorrow and tell me you got with her, 'cause that shit ain't happening."

My partner feigned concern. "Retiring early, again, huh? Like I said back at the other club, Carla's domesticated you. You're a caged Snake."

"No," I protested. "I'm just tired. You know, for somebody who's struck out the last coupla-hundred times he's been at the plate, you sure seem pretty concerned about my home run, you know? Fuck off anyway—do you want me to stick around here and ruin your chances just to prove I still got it?"

"Whatever you gotta tell yourself, man. I think you've got some sort of real, deep attraction to Carla—some sort of longing for meaningful female companionship you've never had before—and that is manifesting itself in the most bizarre, un-Snake-like way possible."

"And what way is that?"

"Loyalty and fidelity, apparently."

I took a long drag off my cigarette before I answered. "Two things. First, I don't even know what fidelity means."

The boss snorted. "In more ways than one."

"And secondly, you're a better pilot than you are a psychiatrist. And that's saying something, because you're a pretty shitty pilot."

"Seems like I struck a nerve, eh, Snake? Well, whatever. You head out and I'll catch up with you tomorrow and tell you how it goes. I'm telling you, man, I got a good feeling. I don't care what you say, I'm not sleeping alone tonight." He slammed back another shot of what looked like tequila.

"Uh-huh," I said as I slid off my barstool. "That's probably true, 'cause there's always more than one guy in the drunk tank."

I didn't listen for his reply and instead pushed through the crowded bar back out into the night's snowy street. I pulled my coat tight around me as I walked, then shook my head. I didn't care too much about my partner trying to needle me about Carla. I was getting some and he wasn't. And the way I figured, it'd be that way for the foreseeable future.

———————————-

The next morning, I woke up in my cheap hotel room around ten, took a long shower, left the room, and walked three blocks down to the closest thing the generic city had to a landmark: The Grand Star Hotel. The Grand Star was only a landmark because it had a historical casino that dated to Yaeger's days as a frontier planet, and *that* only mattered because they still used the casino as a rotating host for the Galaxy Grand Prix Poker Circuit. I didn't give a shit about playing poker, but poker meant money, and money meant good food.

Thing is, good food tends to be expensive, and obviously I was broke as always. Fortunately for me, this wasn't the first time I'd had to solve this problem, so I knew just what to do: I nodded to the doorman, walked into the Grand Star like I belonged, and followed the signs for the elevators. I got in, pressed a floor at random, and got out when the elevator stopped. I looked over the balcony to the restaurant in the lobby fifteen stories below, pleased to see they hadn't stopped serving breakfast yet. With a smile, I strolled down the hall a few doors until I saw one whose holographic display read, Please Do Not Disturb. Taking note of the room's number—1511—I pounded twice on the door, paused a second, and twice more.

"Huh—what—who is it? I thought I put out the do not disturb sign," came a man's groggy voice from inside.

"Holloway Port Security," I barked. "I'm looking for Mister William Travis."

"Huh?"

"Port Security. I'm looking for William Travis," I repeated.

"What? You got the wrong room. I'm Jason Wu."

"That's not what they said downstairs, sir. Room 1611—oh, I'm sorry," I said. "So sorry. I thought I was on the sixteenth floor. My mistake, sir."

The man muttered a curse, and I chuckled as I trotted to the elevator. I took it down and sat down at an empty restaurant table. After a meal of steak and eggs, fresh fruit, pancakes, and a half dozen mimosas, the waiter brought me a substantial check.

I made a show of pretending I didn't have my wallet on me. "This is pretty embarrassing," I told the waiter. "But I must have left my wallet upstairs."

"No problem, sir," he said. "I can charge it to your room."

"Great," I said with a winning smile. "Jason Wu, room 1511, please."

Most of the time I'm the minnow, so whenever I get the chance to be the shark, I never pass it up.

I left the hotel and trudged back to the shipyard in Yaeger's swirling snow, noting—with what began as amusement, then concern—that Michael Ver's very public humiliation at the hands of my boss seemed to be the top story on all the news holos. I started to get the bad feeling that Ver and his people might not be willing to take the L and move on. Given that the weather hadn't improved, and that his crew obviously knew where he'd gotten the coat, there was nothing stopping Liz or any other heavies he had working for him from paying us a visit. That prospect didn't sit well with me. I'd gotten the drop on Liz last night, but I couldn't count on that kind of luck again.

But when I got to the spaceport, I found it empty of both unexpected visitors and film crews. I breathed a sigh of relief and crossed the concrete expanse to our Black Sun 490. The cargo ramp lay open, and I heard the dull hum of the APU over the wind. The boss was already back at the ship. I chuckled, figuring that if he'd gotten lucky like he said he would last night, he'd still be at a hotel somewhere.

"Yo, man you—" I called as I walked up the ramp but stopped mid-sentence when a tall, buxom redhead in her late twenties stepped from the midships into the cargo bay. She flashed a cute knock-em-dead smile and extended a hand, her ruby-hued nail polish gleaming in the cargo bay lights.

"You must be Snake," she said in a perfect lilting accent that marked her as being from somewhere deep in the inner systems—Mars, or maybe even Earth. A rarity indeed in some rathole backwater like Yaeger.

Out of habit and caught completely off guard by what I could only guess was the boss's date from last night, I extended my hand only for her to snatch hers back.

"He told me all about you—said not to talk to you, actually, and certainly not to touch you. He said you're trouble." She gave me a conspiratorial wink that would have sent lesser men to their knees. "Are you trouble?"

"Of a sort," I said with a sly grin that meant *as much trouble as you want me to be, sweetheart.*

The boss appeared through the midships hatch. His eyes met mine and he flashed a triumphant, gloating smile. "Snake, this is Kell," he said gesturing to her unnecessarily. "She came into the bar about a minute after you left. A good trade, I have to say."

I shrugged and fished a cigarette out of my coat. "No argument here. I'd trade her for me."

Kell laughed.

"Don't laugh at his jokes," my partner said in a tone of voice I knew was more directed at me than her. "That only encourages him, and he's incorrigible."

I lit my cigarette and took a drag. "Bustin' out the big words today, I see, now that you got somebody to impress."

"See what'd I tell you," the boss said to Kell. "I told you he was a bitter, sarcastic bastard."

"Don't listen to him, Kell," I said. "Projection's a hell of a thing."

She grinned and shook her head, her striking auburn hair shimmering in the bay lights. "You two are something else."

"That we are," he said.

"So, Kell, what brings you aboard anyway?" I asked. "Whatever stories he's telling you about this rust bucket, let me be the first to say they're all bullshit."

"I wanted to see it," she answered. "I've traveled a lot, but always on the really big ships—starliners, greybacks, that sort of thing. I've been on a few shuttles, but never a real ship like this, and since we're filming the video, well…"

"You're part of the crew? Now that's something, because—"

She chuckled. "Isn't it? I'm not actually on the film crew. I'm one of the backup dancers."

My eyebrows went up and the boss's gloating smile returned.

"Wow. I wouldn't think your boy Ver would like you palling around with the guy who fed him his teeth in front of all his friends," I said.

"Michael's an asshole," Kell said with a dismissive wave. "And I don't work for him directly anyway. I'm on contract with the production company, and if he wants me off the shoot, what do I care? My contract rider pays 110% plus transit on early termination."

"A 'cheaper to keep her' kinda thing?" I asked.

"Pretty much," the boss cut in. "Plus, they told Kell this morning that they're suspending filming for a few days due to an 'unfortunate personal issue' with Ver." He grinned. "I tried to warn him, didn't I?"

I laughed. "Yeah, you did."

"Anyway, Kell and I are almost done here and then we're going to go eat lunch and catch a movie."

"Feel free to tag along," Kell said with apparent sincerity.

"Or not," the boss added with a glare.

I stamped out my cigarette and shook my head.

"Don't you worry, I'm staying here. I never did get that voltage problem fixed, and I may as well take advantage of a quiet ship." While I had a million questions for my boss—namely how the fuck did you pull this one off?—I couldn't very well ask them when Kell was around. Besides, he'd finally met a girl who apparently thought he was a real winner, and there was no reason for me to go along and ruin her illusions.

CHAPTER FOUR

They returned later that night, just as I was about to lock the ship up and head out to grab something to eat. She had a pair of ornate shopping bags under her arm, and he had on a new pair of pants as well as a yellow sweater with a pair of large black stripes across the middle. I had to look twice to make sure it was really him. I'd never seen him wear anything with color save a pair of blue jeans.

"I see you two have been shopping," I said dryly, nodding at his sweater as they walked up the cargo ramp. "The bumblebee collection is a good look for you, bossman."

Embarrassment flashed across his face before he shot me the bird behind Kell's back and mouthed *fuck you*.

"Bumblebee?" Kell asked, confused. "What do you mean? Ooooh, I get it. It's DeSoto," she said, as if the name was supposed to mean something. "It's in style in a big way in the inner systems, but I guess not everybody out here appreciates it."

"That's me, just your average Outer Rim, uncultured lowlife," I said with a smirk. "Of course, we aren't exactly in the inner systems, are we?"

"Shut up. Nobody asked for your fashion advice, Snake. You aren't exactly keeping up with the trends, you know," the boss said.

"Now that is true, I'll admit," I said. "I certainly don't keep up with them the way you do, that's for sure."

My partner's eyes narrowed, and he shook his head. He knew where I was headed. "Don't even start with—"

"Hey, Kell," I said breezily. "Speaking of style, did he show you his watch? It's pretty cool."

Kell's brow wrinkled in confusion. Behind her, the boss pointed at me and made a throat-slashing gesture. I grinned and continued. "Ask him to show you his left wrist. Talk about trendy."

"What's he—"

My partner held out his left wrist with a sigh, and tapped it once. Displayed in faint green digital numbers on his skin was a blinking 1200. Kell's eyebrows went up and a mocking smile flitted across her face before she repressed it.

"Yessiree," I said. "That is a genuine Markos Renroy watch implant. You may have heard about 'em. Used to be the thing on the Outer Rim about ten or twelve years ago. Posh. Very classy. Don't see them too much anymore because now people think they're dumb as hell. Course, some of us thought they were dumb as hell even back then. And what's with the blinking twelves anyway, bossman? It not working anymore?"

"No, it doesn't. And thank you for that little show-and-tell, Snake. Now eat shit and die."

"Any time. Glad I could help."

"C'mon, Kell," the boss said, ignoring me. "You can change onboard and then we'll head out."

"Okay," she said. "I'll change in there." She nodded to the midships and took a bag with her as she went through the hatch.

"Why'd you bring her back here to change for?" I asked. "Most women prefer the comforts of a hotel to a ratty ship. That's a free tip for you, by the way."

"I dunno if you've noticed, Snake, but I'm doing perfectly fine with this all by myself, so you can shove your 'free tips' up your ass, pal. And I had to come back here to drop off my pistol. The place we're going doesn't allow guns." He took off his duster followed by his shoulder holster, which he hung off a junction box on the aft wall. I noticed his black and yellow sweater had bright green sleeves.

"That sweater is the dumbest thing you've ever bought, and I once watched you buy a hold full of licorice-scented candles," I told him.

"They were supposed to appreciate in value," he snapped. "And shut up about the sweater. She liked it, so I bought it."

"Yeah? Well, they didn't, if you remember, and neither will that sweater. But you do your thing, bossman—and I'm serious, for once. No shit, I'm impressed," I said with a nod of my head toward the midships. "I didn't think you had it in you."

"Glad to know I've earned your respect," he deadpanned. "My life is now complete. I can die happy."

"How'd you even get to talking to her?" I asked.

"She came up to me, motherfucker," he said, puffing out his chest. "She was actually in the Club Seventy-Two when it all went down, and she asked around outside till she found some folks who saw which way we went. She really doesn't like Ver, even though she's dancing in the video. No law says you have to like who you work for."

"Imagine that," I said.

The boss's eyes narrowed. "Whatever. I don't care what you say. I'm going to enjoy tonight, just like I did last night, and not even you can ruin it for me, so don't waste your time trying. In the meantime, get whatever work you can done, because the weather's supposed to clear up late, and we're leaving tomorrow before noon to beat the next front."

"Yeah, that sounds fair," I said. "You go out having fun and leave me here to work, just like I have been all day? Fuck that. When are you gonna do some work?"

"I don't recall you doing shit when we were laid up at Rucker Watson's a coupla weeks ago. I've earned my time off."

I shrugged. He had a point. We'd met up with Carla at Rucker Watson's and I hadn't done anything for damn near a week. Except Carla, of course.

"So, like I said, get whatever you can done tonight. If you get a minute, the forward—"

"I'm sorry," Kell interrupted as she came through the midships hatch into the cargo bay, wearing a tight, long-sleeved green dress in place of the jeans she had on earlier. "But I just got a message from the company. They want to do some sort of night shoot for the B unit, so they're sending a car around for me. Shouldn't take too long, though. I'll send you a message on the ship's account when we're done," she told my crestfallen boss.

As if on cue, headlights shone across the spaceport and a brown SUV pulled up outside the ship. The boss's look soured as he watched her get in, but he did manage a wave to her as the SUV pulled away.

"Easy come, easy go," I said as I lit another cigarette.

"She'll be back," he said, staring out into the darkness.

"That's what they all say."

"Shut up, Snake."

"Let's lock up and get something to eat."

"No," he said, shaking his head. "I don't wanna miss her message. Bring me something back, would ya? And be quicker about it than you were last time, aight?"

"What's that supposed to mean?"

"I mean, last time you went out to grab us something to eat you didn't come back until the next afternoon."

"Oh, yeah. That. Well, no promises, but I'll do my best."

"That's less than reassuring," he muttered as he plopped down into a folding chair in the cargo bay.

I laughed and pulled my coat tight around me as I made my way out into the snow.

CHAPTER FIVE

I walked to the little Chinese joint nearest the spaceport, but by the time I got there I was nearly a goddamned popsicle because of the wind, so once I ordered and got our food, I decided to take a cab back. Because Holloway is a nothing-town on a nothing-planet, the cab service was glacially slow, and I didn't get back to the ship for almost an hour.

I arrived to find the Black Sun 490 locked up tight. Kell must have gotten done with her shoot sooner than she expected. I typed in the rear cargo bay door code on the external control panel and let myself inside. The first thing I noticed was a hastily scrawled note on a spare sheet of paper sitting in the folding chair where I'd last seen the boss.

Kell called. Some kind of trouble with Liz. Grand Lotus Hotel, 10006 Gaddis Street.

Well, fuck. I dropped the plastic bag of Chinese food, turned around, and closed and relocked the cargo bay.

I swore under my breath as I trekked across the snowy concrete on what was now a frigid, clear night. A breeze cut through me like an icy blade, sending me into a full-body shiver. I didn't even know where 10006 Gaddis Street was, but even if I did, there was no way I was going to walk there in the freezing temperatures, and given the slow pace of cab service on this godforsaken rock, it seemed likely whatever it was that was going down would be done by the time I got there.

Lucky for the boss, I'm the resourceful type, so I checked out the row of heavy service trucks parked against the spaceport fence. Each was locked, but a white pickup with Holloway Spaceport Maintenance Department stenciled on the side had the keys hidden on top of the driver's side front tire.

Inside the cab, the truck's electric motor showed low charge, but it still said I had an estimated forty minutes of drive time, which seemed better than the nothing I had before. I punched Grand Lotus Hotel into the navigation system and the truck told me I had a fifteen-minute ride ahead. I hit enter and the autopilot zipped me out of the spaceport and down the main drag, and then off toward a garish collection of neon lights that lit the western sky.

I soon found myself outside the wide front steps of a towering black glass and steel hotel whose obsidian facade gleamed pink and green as it reflected light from the downtown restaurants and clubs. Just as I was about to tell the computer to find parking, the hotel's double doors swung open and a familiar figure emerged, running at full tilt down the steps, pistol in his hand.

"What the fuck have you gotten yourself into now, bossman?" I muttered. I rolled down the passenger-side window. "Yo, boss! Over here!"

He looked up in surprise, then sprinted to the truck.

It was just about then a half dozen or so uniformed police spilled out the front door after him.

Great. Just great. Positively out-fucking-standing.

He yanked open the door as I switched the truck to manual mode and hit the accelerator. The back end fishtailed on the ice for a second, but I managed to pull away just before a pair of cops reached my door. I ignored their disappointed shouts as I sped off down a side street.

"Jesus. Fuck, that was good timing," the boss said between ragged breaths.

"What the hell happened?" I asked, frowning as I noted the blue and red lights of police cars in the rearview mirror.

"Fuck if I know," the boss muttered. "I walked into the lobby and asked for Kell. The lady at the desk said she'd call up to the fifth floor where the dance production company had rented all the rooms out. Then a few minutes later she tells me the company says there was nobody with that name up there. So, I figure shit has gone real sour by now, and I take the elevator up. As soon as I step out, Ver and his crew are walking down the hall and Liz sees me. He yells something like 'they're here for Ver, get him' and next thing I know buncha fuckin' private security goons show up outta nowhere and I take off running. They're this close to grabbing me, so I pull out my pistol, fire a shot or two to keep 'em honest and run down five flights of stairs. For some reason, though, there's like a dozen uniforms in the lobby—Holloway PD—and then they're chasing me too. Next thing I know, you're parked out front."

"And you're sure the guys you took a shot at weren't cops? Not plainclothes guys? Please tell me you didn't accidentally shoot at some cops," I muttered, shaking my head.

"No, man, the goon squad on the fifth floor were definitely Liz's boys, not cops."

"And there were a bunch of cops in the lobby? You think that shit is coincidence? No way, man. Kell set you up. She must be—"

The squelch of a police siren interrupted me, followed by a voice over a car-mounted megaphone. "Holloway Police Department! Pull over immediately."

I looked over at my boss, and then down at the truck's instrument panel, which warned me in large red letters that since I wasn't driving in an economical manner I only had about five minutes of battery left. His eyes followed mine.

"Shit," he said.

"Yeah. I didn't know I was gonna be in a police chase tonight, else I'd have borrowed something a little bit more suited. Next time let me know. Let's just pull over and see if we can talk our way out of this, since Liz won't be there to—"

"You have five seconds to surrender your vehicle and cease resisting arrest," the police loudspeaker warned.

"Jesus, they're pushy," the boss said. I took my foot off the accelerator. The truck slowed, but apparently that wasn't enough for the Holloway Police.

"Attempted murder suspects continue to arrest! All units cleared to engage. Suspects, exit the vehicle and surrender your weapons or we *will* shoot!" the cops yelled through the loudspeaker.

The Holloway Police Department clearly didn't have enough to do, so to avoid the crippling meaninglessness of life, they seemed to decide that escalating the situation from "potentially dangerous traffic stop" to "full-fledged gun battle" was the thing to do. No sooner had the announcement ended than the first shot pinged into the rear of the truck, followed by a second round that shattered the rear window.

"Jesus Christ!" the boss yelled, ducking to avoid the next two rounds that completely demolished the back window and punched through the windshield centimeters from my head.

I flinched involuntarily, sideswiping a parked van, then stomped on the accelerator and swerved left down an alley.

"What the fuck, man? Do you really think we're gonna surrender when you're shooting the shit out of us?" I yelled into the rearview mirror.

The truck bounced along uneven pavement as I smashed my way through several garbage cans and a couple of cardboard boxes and knocked off my driver's side mirror on a drainpipe.

"Fuck, Snake, you think you could keep us outta the wall?" the boss asked.

"I'm just driving like you fly," I muttered.

In the rearview mirror, I watched a police car pull into the alley behind us. A hand with a pistol emerged out the passenger-side window.

An earsplitting boom sounded beside me, and I almost ran us into a parked motorbike in the alley. I looked over just in time to watch the boss return fire twice more with his .45. The chances of him hitting anything while shooting out the rear window of a pickup truck doing seventy-five kilometers an hour at night down a bumpy alley were almost nil, but at least the cops backed off a bit.

More shots erupted from the cop car, pockmarking the brick buildings around us.

"Cease fire, or we will respond with deadly force," the loudspeaker shouted, echoing down the alley.

"Motherfuckers, you're already using deadly force!" the boss shouted. He fired another shot and ducked down in the seat to reload.

A warning chime from the dashboard brought my attention briefly off the hazards of screaming down an alley at high speed at night followed by a bunch of homicidal cops, spotlighting still another hazard: the battery was in emergency power mode and would soon shut down.

Shit.

"Just about outta juice, boss!"

"You have got to be fucking with me, Snake. Don't tell me—"

The final building flashed by, and we punched out of the alley perpendicular to a major downtown thoroughfare, all eight lanes full of traffic. I shouted an incoherent curse as we bounced across a concrete sidewalk and into the closest lane.

And right into the side of a blue and white Holloway PD cruiser.

The impact sent me and my partner into the windshield, which—already weakened by the gunfire—gave way and sent us rolling across the pickup truck's hood. I wound up on the roof of the cruiser and the boss on the hood.

My head swam and my ears rang. I tasted blood and my shoulder hurt like hell.

For his part, the boss scrambled off the hood of the police car and yanked open the driver's door, allowing the unconscious cop inside to slide out onto the pavement. My partner disappeared into the cruiser and reemerged with the cop's restricted-use anti-matter rifle. He holstered his pistol and leveled the rifle across the hood. I winced as he fired right back through the cab of our stolen pickup truck and into the police car just as it emerged from the alley.

The whole vehicle forward of the windshield disappeared in a thunderous explosion that sent flaming bits of battery, scraps of metal, and burning plastic bouncing off the nearby buildings. The cop car doors opened and two figures emerged, firing their pistols wildly as they retreated back into the alley.

My partner looked up at me with a grin. "Snake, find us a car."

I scrambled off the roof of the police car and ran across a narrow, snow-covered median into oncoming traffic, slipping and sliding as I did so. Headlights blinded me as tires squealed. I held up my hand to shield my eyes and could just make out a sporty sedan. I ran to the driver's side door, knife in hand.

The door opened, revealing a balding, middle-aged man and his wife.

"Are you all right? I almost hit you out—" he started to say before I wrenched the door open all the way and put my knife in his face.

"Sorry, but I gotta borrow this thing, all right?" I asked.

His wife screamed and leapt out the passenger side. He scrambled across the seat to follow her while I slid inside just as I heard another shot from the anti-matter rifle. Another explosion lit the sky.

"Boss!" I shouted through the open passenger door. "You coming or what?"

He looked over his shoulder, then fired a third shot that went high and sent a cloud of white-hot brick shards exploding off the side of one of the buildings. He darted across the median to the passenger seat, firing a final shot one-handed just before he got inside.

He slammed the door, I mashed the accelerator, and we were off again.

"Do you even know where we're going?" he asked as I weaved us in and out of traffic, ignoring the onboard computer's repeated warnings about hazardous road conditions, unsafe speed, low tire pressure, uneconomic driving, local law enforcement activity, and limited visibility conditions.

"All I know is we're getting the hell away from the crazy murder cops," I said. "And once we do that, we're headed back to the spaceport so we can get the fuck outta here."

"What about Kell?" he asked.

I gave him a look of pure wide-eyed incredulity. "What about her? You cannot be this fucking stupid, boss. Don't you see? This whole deal was a setup, dude! She just so happens to call you and tell you she's in trouble, you show up, and Liz and the cops are waiting for you? You think that's fucking coincidence? 'Cause I don't."

"No. No, she wouldn't do that. She's not like that, Snake."

I rolled my eyes. "What the fuck ever."

"It doesn't even make sense, Snake! Set us up? For what?"

"I dunno, maybe Michael Ver wants to get back at us."

"If he wanted to do that, he knows where the ship is, you dipshit," the boss pointed out.

"I don't know, but there's something fucked up about all this, and the sooner we get outta here, the better. That's all I know," I said.

"She's in trouble, Snake. We can't just leave."

"Like hell we can't! You just met her!"

A police car in the opposite lanes flicked on his lights as we passed. I looked up in the rearview mirror and saw brake lights as the cop bounced his cruiser across the median and into traffic behind us.

"Shit, Snake. Slow down," the boss said. "I knew you were going too fast. Fuck, fuck, fuck."

"Well, if it isn't Mr. Too-Little-Too-Late," I said. "Woulda been nice of you to point that out before our buddy here picked us up."

"Damn it, Snake. Everybody knows when you drive too fast you draw attention to yourself."

"Fine, you tell me how you get away from the scene of a wreck, a shooting, and carjacking in a way that doesn't involve driving fast. In fact, you can take over driving as soon as we lose this asshole." I sped up, but the cruiser gained on us.

Shit.

My partner turned around in his seat to track the pursuing car. "Just let him get up close. I'll take care of him." He patted the black steel and polymer frame of the anti-matter rifle.

"What? A second ago you were worried about my speeding drawing attention to us! You know what else draws attention?" I asked. "You blasting cop cars into flaming wrecks like a goddamn comic-book villain."

"I haven't killed any of 'em yet," he said as he rolled down the passenger-side window.

I snorted. "'Yet.' I'm sure the judge will appreciate that distinction when they play back the dashcam video of you blowing the fuck out of that car in the alley."

"You got a better idea?" he asked, rolling the window back up.

"Yeah," I answered. "Just chill with the rifle for a minute and let me lose him."

I pressed the pedal to the floor and cut across two lanes of traffic and onto the far side of a multi-trailer transfer truck.

"It's not gonna work," the boss said in a singsong voice as the cop appeared behind us, even closer than he was before. "You're not gonna outrun him in this thing."

"Did I not just lose three or four of them in a pickup with no battery?" I asked. "Have a little confidence."

"That was sheer fucking luck, Snake, and you know it."

"Whatever."

Our pursuer continued to gain on us, siren screaming. "Pull over. Pull over immediately."

"I'm telling you, slow down and let him get closer. I got this," the boss said, rolling down the window again and shifting in his seat to get the rifle ready while he kept it inside the car so the cop wouldn't see it.

"Fine, we'll do it your way, but if we go to jail, I'm blaming this whole thing on you, just so you know."

"I wouldn't expect any different, Snake."

I slowed and the cruiser gained on us, pulling to within a meter of our rear bumper. The boss still hadn't taken his shot.

"Jesus Christ, how close do you want him to get?" I asked. "You wanna wait till he gets into the car with us or what? Fuckin' shoot him already!"

"Don't rush me," he said through gritted teeth.

The police car pulled nearly even with us, and the boss ducked out the window, bringing the rifle to bear. I took my eyes off the road to watch.

The cop must have seen him move and known something was up because he slammed on the brakes, and as fast as we were moving, he disappeared like he was in reverse. The boss's shot went wide and hit a tree in the median, turning it into a million flaming splinters and showering the road in burning wood. My partner swore and lined up for another shot. "How the fuck did you miss him so close?" I yelled. "He was right on top of—shit!"

I looked back to the road to see a slow-moving cargo van filling the windshield. The car's computer buzzed a warning, and my heart leapt to my throat as I yanked the wheel sharply right, barely avoiding the van's rear corner and sending both of us tumbling across the cabin. The computer calmly intoned "Autopilot override for traction stability" as the car whipped back to the left, slinging us back across the car. There was a clatter from the passenger side followed by a thunk from the rear of the car as the rear passenger-side wheel ran over something.

"Fucking shit! Fuck, fuck, fuck, goddamn it!" the boss shouted as he stuck his head out the window.

"What? What was that?" I asked as I took the wheel and switched the control back to manual mode, keeping my eyes on the road ahead and straining to see out past my headlights.

"Fuuuuuuck," he said, drumming on the dash.

The rifle was nowhere to be seen. "Oh, no. Tell me you didn't. Was that the rifle I just ran over?" I asked, shaking my head.

"If you would have paid attention to the road like you're supposed to do when you drive, it wouldn't have happened!" he shouted.

"If you wouldn't have missed a shot when the target was an arm's length away, I wouldn't have had to keep watching!"

"You act like you've never missed an easy shot," he snapped.

I swerved around a motorcycle and noticed the police car approaching quickly on the driver's side. I jerked left and the cruiser backed off, but not by much.

"Fuckin' great," I said. "Now what?"

"I've still got my pistol," the boss said.

"Okay, well that's nice, except I'm pretty sure he's gonna stay on my side, since he doesn't know you dropped the fucking rifle out the goddamn window. And if you think I'm going to let you shoot across me, you got another thing coming."

"I'll handle it," he said. "But you watch the road this time and not me, got it? Keep us as nice and straight as you can."

I mumbled a curse but kept my focus on the road. Fortunately, the traffic had thinned out by this point, leaving the dark road empty besides us and our sirened pursuer. I kept the pedal down and positioned us in the dead center of the road.

The boss climbed into passenger-side window, gripping the inside of the roof with his right hand to keep from falling out while the wind whipped around him. He pulled his revolver from his holster with an unsteady left hand. My eyes flicked between him and the road ahead.

This motherfucker was really going to try to make a left-handed shot with a pistol, at night, out of a moving vehicle, backward across the roof, shooting at yet another moving vehicle—after he'd just missed at point-blank range with a fucking shoulder cannon.

He didn't have a chance in hell.

The wind rushing through the cabin was almost loud enough to cover up the two gunshots, but it wasn't loud enough to mask the sound of screeching tires and crunching metal.

I looked in the rearview mirror to see the police car swerving out of control, sparks flying from the front passenger-side wheel. The cruiser spun around at high speed, bounced across the median, and slammed into a ditch on the other side of the road.

The boss dropped back inside and re-holstered his pistol. He rolled up the window and leaned back in his seat, folding his hands behind his head.

"No fucking way," I said, mouth hanging open in amazement.

He grinned. "No sweat."

"You couldn't do that again in a million years."

"Doesn't matter," he said. "I only had to do it once."

CHAPTER SIX

It took us nearly two hours of sticking to back roads to get back to the Holloway Spaceport, but at least we avoided any further trouble with the police. I was just happy I'd managed to convince my partner we had to move the ship if nothing else, since Ver and Liz both knew who we were and where the ship was, and if the cops came calling, they'd have no qualms about ratting us out. My hope was that once we got airborne, my boss would see reason, lose his chivalric streak, and blast us off Yaeger never to return.

"We got a serious problem, Snake," the boss said as we pulled through the gates. He pointed across the frozen concrete to our Black Sun 490. The running lights were on, and the lack of snow around the ship told me its APU had been powered up for some time. The cargo ramp was down, and I could just make out a figure moving around outside the ship, backlit by the cargo bay lighting.

"Who is that? What the fuck is going on?" I asked.

"I dunno, but let's find out."

I punched the accelerator, and we sped across the tarmac.

"Uh, Snake, what are you trying to…"

He didn't finish, and I didn't answer. As our headlights painted the ship, a pair of figures walking from a distant row of forklifts toward our Black Sun 490 cast long shadows across the near-abandoned spaceport. One was a muscular Asian man I didn't recognize, but the other was all too familiar—our favorite tattooed fixer, Liz.

He and the Asian guy shared a look of bewildered shock, then took off in separate directions. I already disliked Liz the most, so I kept the car aimed at him. Pinned in the dark by my headlights, he hesitated for a moment, then reached for his waistband.

Bad decision.

I caught up to him just as we pulled even with the ship, and he had just enough time to give me a wide-eyed look of horror before I hit him. The impact rolled him onto the hood and smashed him into the windshield, sending a spiderweb of cracks across it. Above me, I heard a *clunk-thunk-clunk* that told me he'd rolled across the roof, and then a dull thud as he fell off the trunk and onto the snowy pavement.

I slammed on the brakes, and the boss and I jumped out of the car. He fired a shot into the dark to discourage Liz's companion, and I sprinted up the cargo bay ramp—only to literally run right into Kell. She tripped and fell backward, having just enough time to brace herself before she landed, and I came down on top of her. I have to say, there are worse places to land.

But in the moment, the only thing going through my head were two obvious questions: what the fuck is going on and what the fuck is she doing on our ship?

I scrambled off her, drawing my knife as she got to her feet, steeling myself for the possibility that I was going to have to stab her if she reached for a gun. Instead, she avoided my knife and leapt into my arms, hugging me tightly and burying her head in my shoulder.

"Oh my god," she sobbed. "It's you. Oh god, I'm so thankful. I can't—they, they were going to—"

While I was trying to process all the mixed signals I was getting from both her and my body, I heard a very this-had-better-be-fucking-good throat clearing behind me.

Kell pulled her head off me, looked over my shoulder, and was out of my arms in an eyeblink.

I turned to face the boss, who was now on the receiving end of the same treatment I'd gotten, which you'd think would have made him happy, but of course he was a poor sport, as always. He hugged Kell, but the look he gave me was one of pure suspicion.

"They'll be back," she said to the boss. "I'm telling you, they're going to come back. You can't let them get me!"

"Nobody's going to get you, baby," he said, patting her back. "But we have to get out of here."

I couldn't believe what I'd just heard. "Whoa, whoa. Say what? You don't mean we as in we're taking her with us, do you? Because that's insane. The only reason 'they' would come back for her is because she's working with them in the first place!"

Kell shot me a wounded look. "They kidnapped me, Snake!"

"Like hell," I snapped. "You just weren't expecting us to be here. It's just pure coincidence that I showed up in time—"

"Snake, we're taking off," the boss said, with a voice that told me his rusted steel trap of a mind had snapped shut. "We'll sort this out in the air."

"What? You can't even—"

It was at that point that I realized, comically late, that our cargo bay had a standard sixteen-meter-by-three-meter steel shipping container in the bay that hadn't been there before. The nondescript red-and-blue-painted container could have been any one of millions, save for the fact that it had an intricate selection of multiple locks on the outside. It was a testament to Kell's physique and emotion that it hadn't been the first thing I'd seen.

For his part, the boss seemed to have had the same realization, as he stopped mid-stride, looked the container up and down, then turned to me.

"What is that?"

"Don't ask me, ask her," I said, pointing an accusing finger at Kell.

"I don't know," she said, eyes wet. "I don't know. When Liz found out I'd been hanging out with—" Kell froze.

Liz appeared out of the dark at the base of the cargo ramp, lit ominously in red by our stolen car's taillights. He looked considerably worse for the wear: eyes unfocused, left arm twisted at an odd angle, and bleeding from a gash across his head.

But what immediately drew my attention was the pistol in his right hand.

It must have also drawn the boss's attention, because he squeezed off two quick shots in Liz's direction.

Both of which missed, of course.

Liz fired back, sending a slug pinging through the cargo bay and another two snapping uncomfortably close to my head. Kell screamed, the boss swore, and I dove behind an empty metal bin we used to hold spare parts. I hit the deck hard and stayed put, cursing the boss's poor marksmanship.

The boss fired again and Liz shouted, but whether it was a cry of pain or anger, I couldn't tell. So, like a dumbass, I stuck my head around the side of the bin and almost got it taken off by Liz's parting shot. Clutching his side with his damaged left arm, the goon stumbled back down the ramp and collapsed into the snow, still bathed in the red taillight glow.

"Snake!" the boss yelled. "Close the ramp! I'm getting us outta here!"

I smashed the bay door button with my palm and sprinted past Kell toward the midships, hot on the heels of my boss.

A quick look at the midships computer cabinet told me whoever had been getting the ship prepped prior to us showing up hadn't bothered to power up the turret, but the rest of the ship appeared ready for takeoff.

"Boss!" I shouted. "I dunno about preflights, but everything back here is good to go!"

"All right," he said as he slid into the cockpit. "I think we're gonna abbreviate preflights this trip, Snake."

He flipped a few switches and I heard the muffled roar of our retro rockets, along with the hum of the anti-grav units. I took one last glance at the display to make sure nothing was about to explode. "Still good," I told him. "Let's get the fuck off Yaeger, please."

He didn't answer, but the ship ascended like the world's quickest elevator as he punched the anti-grav system.

"What are—" Kell began.

"You," I hissed, stabbing a finger in her face. "Sit right there." I pointed to the couch that passed as our only piece of furniture onboard. "And don't fucking move," I whispered so the boss couldn't hear me. "He may have bought whatever shit you're trying to pull, but I haven't."

Her pale face went even paler, but she sat on the couch as instructed.

I dropped down in the turret, powering it up and running through initial preflight recalibrations from pure muscle memory. As I did so, I couldn't help but shake my head as I tried to make sense of the last five minutes.

Basically, as best I could figure, the situation was this: somebody, for reasons unknown, was trying to steal our ship to move their cargo of only-god-knows-what to only-god-knows-where. And then, on top of that, for some other unknown reason—likely my boss's long sexual dry spell—we were willingly taking one of the would-be ship thieves with us as a guest.

I heard radio chatter from the cockpit, which ended with the boss saying, "No, you don't get it. I understand I don't have clearance, I just don't care."

"Spaceport control?" I asked from the turret.

"No," he called back. "Yaeger insys, believe it or not."

"Shit. What do they want? Insys doesn't usually give a rat's ass about flight clearances."

"I think it may have a little something to do with our fun with the police back there," he said.

"What did you do with the police?" Kell asked.

"Nothing you need to worry about," I said, just as the main engines kicked on and we rocketed clear of Yaeger's atmosphere.

"Where are we going?" Kell asked.

"Well, for right now, we're headed to the Y-44 jump point, because it's closest and I wanna get out of system before insys decides they want to help out the Holloway PD," the boss replied from the cockpit. "After that, it will depend on whatever cargo it is we've got back there."

"And whatever your story is," I muttered to Kell under my breath.

What I didn't understand then was that the story went so deep that by the time we got to the bottom of it, we'd be lucky if we could climb back out again.

CHAPTER SEVEN

A tense hour later, our Black Sun 490 cruised the nav lane on autopilot toward the Y-44 point, and the three of us stood in the cargo bay beside the mystery container. We'd already examined the locks on the front and noticed a strange addition to the front of the container, which now faced the bulkhead between the cargo bay and the crew area. The addition consisted of a series of locked metal boxes that seemed to be switchboxes or maintenance panels. A few had vents and green-glowing status lights that reminded me of a refrigeration unit, but the system didn't have the sort of loud APU common to refrigerated containers, and as far as I could tell, didn't make any noise at all aside from a high-pitched electrical hum. The only writing on them was an unfamiliar manufacturer's mark: Ito-Tenson. The container had no other markings save for the fading logo of one of the big interstellar shipping lines, but it been painted over years ago, judging by the state of the container.

"So, Kell, care to explain all this?" I asked, not bothering to keep the suspicion out of my voice.

She sat on an empty spare parts crate and put her head in her hands. "It's my fault," she said between tears. "Liz had been following you two already after the fight in the club, and I guess he saw us together. Anyway, he didn't say anything about it until tonight. He had one of the other dancers send me the message about coming back for another shoot, but when I got there it was just him and some of his guys. Liz told me he knew I'd been with you." She nodded at my partner. "And then he asked if I could get into the ship. And I'd seen the code to open the cargo ramp, so—"

"So you told him?" I shouted. "You just went and told him so Liz could steal the ship? Are you—"

"He had a gun on me," Kell sobbed.

"Calm the fuck down, Snake, and let her talk," the boss said, and the look in his eyes told me he wasn't going to ask twice.

"So he told me I had to call and tell you to come. He said I had to get both of you, but I was so scared when I called I forgot. He was pissed when the front desk told him only you showed up."

"Snake was out getting some food," my partner told her. "And I wasn't waiting."

"I swear to god, I didn't know what he was planning," she said, tears streaming down her face. "But when he heard you showed up, he and some of his guys tossed me in the trunk of the car. When they let me out, they had the crate loaded and then you two showed up before they could finish whatever they were doing. I'm so sorry." She sobbed again, and the boss sat down on the crate next to her and put his arm around her. I narrowed my eyes. I have to admit, I felt a little guilty about how hard I'd been on her, but for a reason I couldn't quite put my finger on, I couldn't bring myself to totally buy her story.

"It's okay," he said. "It's all right now. Liz is out of the picture."

"Did Liz say what was in the container?" I asked.

She shook her head.

"Are you sure? Because—" A glare from the boss cut me off mid-sentence.

"Tell you what, Kell," the boss said as he rubbed her shoulder. "Go stretch out on the couch in the cabin, and Snake and I will see if we can figure out what we've got onboard. I'll join you in a minute."

She nodded and made her way through the cargo bay hatch into the midships, and the boss pressed the switch to close it behind her.

"What the fuck is with you, Snake?" he growled, eyes lit with anger. "She's had a pretty rough fucking night and doesn't need you giving her the third degree."

"I dunno, bossman. Something bothers me about it. I just—something's not right."

"Jesus, Snake, get a grip, man. Sometimes things just are what they are."

"Well, if it is what she says it is, it won't be any big deal if I keep asking her about it until—"

"Until what?"

"Until she tells us the truth."

"Snake," the boss warned.

"What? I don't buy her story."

"It's not a story!" he shouted.

"Like hell it isn't," I said. "If it was a straight random ship theft, why pick us? Why would they bother to bring her along? How did they know where—"

"Enough, Snake," the boss cut in. "Just shut the fuck up for a minute, all right? Jesus, you're paranoid that everybody's out to get you, aren't you?"

"It's the only reason I've lived as long as I have."

"Oh yeah? I'd attribute it to that old saying about god looking out for drunks and fools."

I snorted. "And which am I supposed to be?"

"Both."

Touché.

"Well, you think whatever you want, bossman, but I say the first place we land, the first thing we do is get rid of this box here." I stabbed a finger at the container. "And the next thing we do is get rid of her." I pointed toward the midships.

"Go fuck yourself, Snake."

"That's more your style, don't you think? At least until she came along."

He glowered and his right hand balled into a fist. "Snake, get the bolt cutters, get this thing open, and shut the fuck up before I beat your stupid ass," he said. He shook his head and stomped off toward the midships.

"Fine," I told the empty bay. "But don't come crying to me when this ends in tragedy."

I searched the bay for the bolt cutters, finding them underneath a pile of oily rags that looked like a fire warning poster. I trotted over to the container and put the cutters' massive jaws around the first padlock. I squeezed the handles together, the same way I'd done a thousand times before when cutting off my own locks that I'd forgotten the combination to or other people's locks whose combinations I'd never known. This time, though, the bolt cutters refused to bite through the lock. I frowned and tried again, straining to close the handles until I thought I would pass out. I set the bolt cutters aside and took a moment to regain my breath, kneeling to examine the lock.

I noticed the writing on the slate-gray lock: *Everlock G Series. Black diamondite forged.* I swore under my breath as I checked the other two padlocks. Both of them were diamondite as well, and a fourth lock was a one-time lock that looked suspiciously like an explosive anti-tamper bolt I'd once seen nearly take someone's arm off in a previous job.

Whoever had packed whatever it was in this container didn't want anybody getting into it, that was for sure.

I sighed and walked back to the cargo bay hatch and pressed the open button. The hatch did not slide open, meaning it was electronically locked from the other side.

I banged on the door. "Yo, boss! Open this fucking hatch up. We got a problem."

I heard muttered curses and my boss's heavy footfalls. The hatch slid open and the boss greeted me. His face was flushed and he looked like he'd just put his shirt back on.

Behind him, I saw Kell smoothing out her long red hair and pulling her dress back onto her right shoulder. I had the realization that even if I had solid proof of whatever it was that made me uneasy about Kell, there was no way I was going to win. Kell had my partner right where she needed him. And to be honest, I had to admit to myself that it was at least partially my fault.

My consistent success with women that I'd always rubbed in his face was finally coming back to bite me. I was suddenly sorry I'd stolen Nasra from him on Dunbar, and for Carla. And making out that one time with that girl from the club he liked at Sitorai Safed. I regretted that time I cockblocked him with that one blonde chick on Mileto VII. And when I made fun of him that time he got epically rejected on Paris V. And for Jamila, on Camus. And also that time I went home with those two brunettes on Halifax Station when he went back to the ship with nobody.

Okay, so maybe I didn't actually regret that last one, but still.

"What is it?" he asked, in a tone of voice that told me I was lucky he'd even opened the hatch.

"The locks are black diamondite, man. Not gonna get through them. And one of them is an explosive bolt, I think. We're gonna have to rent something when we land. That fucking crate may as well be a bank vault."

"Jesus, Snake. I gotta do all the thinking around here? Use the fucking plasma cutter and get it open. If you're worried about the explosive bolt, cut open the side."

"Maybe you should do a bit more thinking about that. Plasma cutter's broke, remember?"

"Shit."

"Yeah. Surprised you didn't remember that. Something else on your mind?"

"Shut up," he said. "Try those power shears we use to—"

"I don't think you should do that," Kell said from the couch.

"Oh really?" I asked, looking past the boss to stare daggers at her. "And just why is that?"

"Because Liz said it was something dangerous."

"Nice of you to tell us that after I already tried to get it open," I said.

"I forgot," she sighed, and for a moment I thought she might cry again. "I just remember Liz telling the other guy he was with to make sure it's locked up tight because he wouldn't want 'it getting out.' That's what he said."

"Doesn't want it getting out?" I asked. "What the hell is he shipping? A fucking tiger?"

"I already told you, I don't know," Kell said.

"It doesn't matter," the boss said. "The power shears probably wouldn't work on steel that thick anyway. We'll figure it out when we land."

"Where are we going, anyway?" Kell asked.

I was about to cut in with you sure are pretty damn inquisitive for a stowaway, but the boss answered first.

"San Pierre. It's a shithole, but it's close, their insys is lazy as hell, and their docking fees are cheap. I don't want to fly around too long with whatever we got until I know we aren't gonna get arrested after some random scan."

"First smart thing you've said all day," I told him.

"Glad I have your approval," he said. "In the meantime, why don't you get to work cleaning up the bay?"

I rolled my eyes. "Since when do you get to tell me—"

An alarm sounded from the cockpit.

"What's that?" Kell asked as the boss scrambled past her to the cockpit.

"That," I said as I dropped down into the turret, "is the radar warning. We just picked up someone flying with a nonstandard IFF signal."

"What does that mean?"

"It's either pirates or the cops."

I checked the radar. My targeting system could only pick out a hazy signal at the distance, but I did see it was closing on us from behind at high speed. I had the uncomfortable feeling of someone watching me, and I looked up to find Kell staring down at me from the open hatch.

"Which is it? Pirates or the cops?" she asked.

"I dunno. I was about to ask you the same question."

"What's your deal, Snake? Why are you such an asshole to me?"

"Two reasons. First, I'm that way to everybody. You can ask flyboy if you want. He'll tell you."

"And the second reason?"

"I think you're lying to us, and even worse, I think you're gonna break my boy's heart when he finally figures that out."

A flash of anger sparked in her eyes. "That's three reasons. But, I promise, I'm not going to break his heart."

I checked the incoming radar blip again as I answered. "And what about the part about you lying?"

I looked up, but she was gone.

CHAPTER EIGHT

Twenty minutes later, our pursuer had drawn close enough for my targeting radar to give me a good return. The incoming ship was a Hradi light fighter showing valid Yaeger insys transponder codes.

"Yo, boss, I'm showing an insys IFF. Yaeger local. And he's got those engines on at full burner, judging by the heat sig."

"Yeah," he called from the cockpit. "I've got us moving as fast as we can. I don't wanna strip guns and shield power unless we have to."

"How long to the jump point?" I asked.

"Looks like, uh… two minutes. Jump calc is basically done. Shouldn't take more than fifteen seconds once we get to the jump point."

"Well, that's good," I said as I ran through a basic calculation. "But based on closing speed, that's gonna be cutting it real close."

"What's he gonna do? He hasn't even reached out over comms yet. He isn't just gonna pull up and start shooting."

"Do you remember the Holloway PD, boss?"

"This is insys. They're different."

"Different in that they fly instead of drive. Still just as likely to blast our ass into pieces for no good reason."

"Black Sun 490, Black Sun 490," a hard female voice called over the comm link. "Cease travel and come to full stop immediately. You are wanted for questioning regarding an incident on Holloway Spaceport, Yaeger."

"Last calling station, you're coming in broken and unreadable. Say again," the boss called. We'd learned a long time ago that the easiest way to buy time was just to pretend you didn't understand what was going on.

"Black Sun 490. I say again. Stop your movement and come to full stop and standby for navigation data upload. You will accompany me back to Yaeger."

I slewed my turret and used my zoom magnification to get a better look at our pursuer.

She flew the old insys standard Hradi light fighter—maneuverable but undergunned. Unfortunately for us, Hradis were also quite fast. As quickly as she was closing, we'd be inside gun range in seconds.

"Last calling station, say again. You're still coming in broken," the boss radioed back, still sprinting toward the jump point.

"Black Sun 490, cut the bullshit. You are wanted for questioning in conjunction with a serious crime."

"Whatever it was, we didn't do it, and if we did do it, we didn't mean it, and if we did, they deserved it," the boss told the insys pilot. "Doesn't matter anyway, 'cause we're outta here. Later."

"Wait," Kell said from her place above me in the midships. "Do you mean that—"

"Jumping in three, two, one," the boss said from the cockpit.

The world slid away in the disorienting feeling of weightlessness and blur of colors that marked a jump. We emerged on the other side of the jump point in San Pierre into heavy nav lane traffic.

"I… I think I'm gonna be sick," Kell said from the couch.

"Whatever mess you make, you're cleaning up," I warned. "And don't even think about hanging over the edge of the turret, because if you throw up on me, I swear to fucking god I will—"

"Snake, shut up," my partner snapped from the cockpit.

"I—I've traveled all over," Kell stammered. "But I've never felt like this. My stomach…"

"The bigger the mass, the smoother the jump," the boss explained. "You can hardly even feel it on those big starliners you're used to, Kell. Just close your eyes and picture punching Snake in the face. That always calms me down."

"Aww, that's nice that you let me live in your head like that," I said. "Plenty of empty space up there to spread out."

"Instead of making smart-ass comments, Snake, how about you keep up a scan? We got a lot of traffic out here, and there could be a wolf mixed in with all these sheep."

"Hey, I've been scanning. You just do your part and don't fly us into anything," I said.

"Won't the insys follow us?" Kell asked.

"Nah, insys isn't UNF," the boss said. "And insys crossing system boundaries is how wars get started. No, the Yeager clowns will stay in Yaeger, and, as far as I can remember, Snake and I are clean in San Pierre."

I furrowed my brow as something came to mind.

"Boss, did we ever take care of the—"

"More or less," my partner said. "Besides, that was like a year or two ago anyway. They won't even remember that. Probably."

———————————

As we picked our way around massive starliners, a pair of old San Pierre insys craft, and several other independent shippers like ourselves, a small, boxy fighter caught my eye. The flashy purple and red paint job marked it as a bounty hunter, and the way it seemed to hug the side of a giant Yokohama bulk freighter as it closed the distance to us made me think it was up to something. In my experience, the "something" bounty hunters usually got up to was somebody else's violent death.

"Yo, Kell, you got a babysitter out here in San Pierre?"

"Huh? What are you talking about?"

"I mean, is any of the crew you're working with expecting to meet you here? 'Cause I think we got company."

"I'm not working with anybody!" she shouted. "If there's somebody out here, I don't know who it is."

"Uh-huh, sure," I muttered.

"Whatcha see out there, Snake?" the boss asked. "We got no bounty, at least not that I'm tracking. Nobody should be looking for us out here. I mean, shit, we just left Yaeger a few hours ago, so it can't be those bastards. Besides, nothing we did would be worth their insys or Holloway PD siccing a hunter on us."

"I know that," I said. "But that doesn't change the fact that I got a little purple fighter—Marion F class, maybe?—out here with a pilot that thinks he's slick 'cause he's creeping up off our five o'clock low using a bulk freighter for cover. I can't even get a good return on him for ID purposes."

"Huh. I think I can pick him out up here. Hold on." As the boss cycled through menu options in the cockpit, I zoomed in with my gun camera and kept my eyes on the purple Marion.

"He'll be in missile range soon, if he isn't already, bossman," I warned.

"I don't get it," Kell said, her voice quivering. "I thought you guys said you were clean. Why would you be worried about a bounty hunter?"

"Call it professional caution. I'm going to see if I can get his ID and give him a call and figure out what the hell's going on," the boss answered.

As I watched with growing unease, the bounty hunter cut his throttle and let the Yokohama pass over him, hiding him completely. He'd either realized he was tracking the wrong target or he was doing a final heads-down verification in his cockpit before he came out guns blazing.

"Boss, I think he's coming for us," I said.

"Is he going to—" Kell began, but the boss's radio call cut her off.

"Bounty hunter license number 011-558-9931," he said. "This is Black Sun 490 in the nav lane headed for nav point four. It looks like you're trying to get into position on us. Care to tell us what this is all about?"

There was no response.

I frowned. The hunter had still not emerged from under the Yokohama, meaning he'd matched speed and was using it for continuous cover. Shit was about to go down.

"Bounty hunter, this is Black Sun 490, I say again, tell us what's going on?" the boss called again.

"You know what's going on," a voice responded. "I got a contract to run—contract 455A-Z3, placed in Novokalingrad. Sector wide."

My heart skipped a beat. What the hell had we done to earn a sector-wide bounty?

"I think you got the wrong guys," the boss responded with more confidence than I would have. "We haven't done anything to—"

"It isn't on you," the hunter replied. "It's on your cargo. So dump it and I'll be on my way."

"Sounds like a plan to me," I said. "It isn't ours anyway, and I could give two shits about what happens to Liz's stuff."

"Don't! Not here," Kell pleaded, voice panicked. I had to admit, if she was acting, she was doing a great job. "If Liz or whoever he's working with find out it's blown up or something, they'll come after us all. And you two can run, but I don't have a ship. I'm a dancer. This isn't what I do!"

"I'm pretty sure Liz is a) small time and b) dead," I said through clenched teeth, keeping my gun trained on where I thought the bounty hunter would emerge from under the Yokohama.

"If you've got everything figured out, why'd some guy with a bounty on you show up out of nowhere? Seems like 'pretty sure' isn't real reassuring, coming from you," she snapped.

"She's right, Snake," the boss said. "We need to find out what's going on or else we'll never get clear of it."

"And you think digging deeper into it will?" I asked.

"That's not what I meant. I mean—"

"Black Sun 490, whatcha thinking in there?" the bounty hunter said over the radio. "You're running out of time to decide, and if I have to decide, it ain't gonna be pretty."

"I don't dump my cargo for anybody," my pilot radioed back. This was straight bullshit of course, as we'd dumped our cargo to avoid getting hulled a dozen times, but in our world it's best to play the tough guy right up until you can't. "And you can't make me," the boss continued. "That's straight piracy. We got two insys fighters ninety seconds away anyway. You gonna try to pull this shit here?"

"It's your funeral," the bounty hunter called back.

He darted out from underneath the Yokohama, and I trained my guns on him with my right hand while cycling through the targeting frequencies on the countermeasure VDU with my left.

"The motherfucker's headed our way, boss," I called. "It's party time."

The boss punched the afterburners, sending us rocketing alongside a hulking Lockheed Starskipper so close that the ship's proximity alarms blared. Other traffic in the nav lane began moving away, with smaller ships accelerating farther down the lane and the more massive ones slowly heeling out into deep space.

"He's got a lock!" the boss shouted.

"I got it, I got it," I said as I scanned through the frequencies. I found the correct one, punched the countermeasures button, and checked the range to the hunter. I smiled. He was still out of gun range, but he wouldn't be for long if he kept closing.

"What's going on?" Kell asked, panic in her voice.

I didn't answer and neither did the boss, who preferred to call for help instead. "Flash traffic on the net! Flash traffic on the net! San Pierre insys security, San Pierre insys security, this is Black Sun 490 in the main nav lane on course to point four. We've got a pirate—bounty license 011-558-9931—that has ordered me to drop my cargo and is now attacking. Need assistance!" he called over the comms as the Starskipper we'd been using for cover pulled away from us.

"This is San Pierre insys. Last calling station, you're coming in broken and unreadable. Say again," an unconcerned voice replied.

If there's one fucking thing I hate about how god runs the universe, it's his use of situational irony.

"Man, fuck those guys," the boss muttered from the cockpit and pulled us into a steep dive.

I broke another missile lock and watched space light up at our four o'clock as a missile lost its target and detonated on our countermeasures. I glanced down at my targeting radar.

The hunter was in range.

I worked him over with a long burst before another dive from the boss between a pair of bulk haulers took the bounty hunter out of my cone of fire. The hunter responded with shots of his own that ate into our rear shields, but the boss rolled us over and the purple fighter reappeared, close behind and high.

"Get bent, fucker," I told the bounty hunter through clenched teeth. My shots arced against his shields and scored a mark on his right wing.

He slipped right, filling the space between us with red laser fire as he did so, and taking our rear shields down to what my VDU told me was 5%. He juked away from my next burst, and a sudden sharp bank to starboard threw off my aim. Angry, distracting chatter from other traffic filled my station, and I switched off comms, trying to keep my focus on the hunter.

Our ship shook and the cabin lighting flickered. I glanced up to see Kell looking down at me, her face pale and her knuckles white as she held on to the turret ring.

"Shit!" the boss called as we pulled into a steep climb. I slewed the turret around, trying to find our attacker and was treated to an up-close view of a Yangtzee C-7 that must have been trying to avoid getting caught in the crossfire but had instead maneuvered right in front of us. The C-7 was so close I could count the rivets on its starboard side. Our shields arced against one another as we came perilously close to a collision.

"Fucking Christ, man, watch out!" I shouted.

"You just stick to gunning and let me fly, how about it?" the boss snapped.

More laser fire flashed around us, and the ship shook again, this time accompanied by a chirping alarm from the midships computer cabinet.

"What's that?" Kell asked.

"Nothing to worry about—yet," I grunted.

I slewed my turret back around just in time to catch a flash of purple as he pulled up and out of my cone of fire.

Another Starskipper, this one with a wide blue stripe down the centerline, passed underneath us. The boss cut the engines and hit the thrust reversers, rocking me forward almost into my gun display screen and the sending the ship shuddering to a halt. Kell lost her grip above me, and tumbled down into the turret with me just as our bounty-hunting friend zipped out from underneath the Starskipper, not expecting us to be at an almost dead stop above the larger ship.

Any other day and I'd have had him dead to rights and probably been able to hull him, but Kell landed on top of me, her knees smashing my face into my right VDU, and her left hand on my left shoulder as she tried to steady herself. Normally, I'd be all about a pretty redhead down in the turret with me—even one I didn't quite trust and who'd been sleeping with my boss, to be honest—but this wasn't the most opportune time.

My burst went wide. The bounty hunter pulled into a tight loop, and I lost him, but I knew what was coming next. We were sitting ducks, and our Black Sun wasn't exactly the fastest ship off the line, which meant we were going to take a pounding right in the nose while the boss struggled to get us back up to speed, all because my boss's girl couldn't do as instructed and stay seated on literally the only piece of furniture in the whole goddamn ship.

Kell scrambled back out of the turret, kicking me in the head as she did so, and I watched our forward shields march down to nothing as we took repeated hits while the boss frantically tried to increase engine power to get us out of the way.

The boss rolled us along our x axis, and I managed to get off a burst at the bounty hunter just as his shots punched through our shields, shorting out our targeting radar and lighting up a cluster of warning lights on my VDU.

Another burst or two like that and I'd have a lot more to worry about than warning lights.

As we accelerated, I laid a long burst on him that drove the bounty hunter into a dive. I ignored the overheat warning flashing on my gun status VDU and kept the pressure up, taking his topside shields to nothing and then sawing off the outer edge of his left wing. The bounty hunter rolled right, trying to get away, but in the tangle of ships taking evasive action, he'd lost track of a slope-sided Gellner Astrohauler—which he promptly rolled into.

The lumbering freighter's shields arced white for a moment before they smashed the small purple fighter into a brief fireball and an expanding cloud of glowing shards.

"Not the best way to do it, but I'll take it," the boss called from the cockpit.

"Any fight you can walk away from is a good fight," I answered, wiping the sweat off my forehead.

I flicked my comms station back on. Insys was calling. "Black Sun 490, this is San Pierre insys security," the same voice as earlier asked over the comms. "I think we got our comms problem fixed from earlier. Are you in need of assistance?"

"No. We got it. But thanks for all the help," the boss called back, voice dripping with sarcasm. "I'll be sure to call the next time I don't need anything."

"You do that," the voice said with a chuckle. "San Pierre insys out."

"Fuckin' insys," the boss muttered. "They're never around when you need 'em, and then the one time they are, they still don't do shit."

"Are—are we—is it over?" Kell stammered.

"Yeah," I said as I stood out of my turret to shut off the chirping alarm in the midships computer cabinet. "It's over. And next time, stay on the fucking couch," I told her in a quiet, threatening voice so the boss wouldn't overhear.

"What's the damage look like back there?" the boss asked over his shoulder as we accelerated back into the nav lane's normal traffic.

"I overheated the left capacitor bank," I said. "So, gun one will only fire in degraded mode, but I think new fuses and a simple reset will fix it." I scanned the list of warnings and sensor errors on the midships computer cabinet again. "Other than that, it looks pretty minor except—"

"Except the gravimetric sensor?" he interrupted.

"Yep."

"Yeah, we took a pretty good shot forward— after you missed the point-blank shot I set you up for, by the way."

"Yeah? Well, shit happens," I said, glaring at Kell. She wouldn't meet my eyes.

CHAPTER NINE

We made it to San Pierre and got clearance to land without further trouble, although I kept up a wary scan the whole way, just in case. San Pierre itself was a hot, miserable, dry, dusty planet whose sole claim to fame was that it was the only inhabitable place in the Y-44 system that wasn't a corporate-owned asteroid mining rig. I scoped out the spaceport as we descended. It hadn't changed much since the last time I'd been through San Pierre, meaning it was likely still the same tiny backwater with high prices, shitty food, and bad booze.

"So, what's the plan, boss?" I asked.

"Simple. Me and Kell are gonna get to an FTL comms terminal and see what's on the net about this fucking bounty on our heads, and you're gonna crack open that container and see what it is we've got. If it turns out to be something we can offload here, we do it. I don't give a rat's ass if we have to do it cheap—I just want to be done with it."

"What if somebody's down there, looking for us?" Kell asked.

"Doubtful," he answered as we made our final descent. "San Pierre's a pretty good way off the beaten track, and most bounty hunters wouldn't want to waste their time hanging out in a shitty place like this unless they knew for sure their target was going to show up, and chances are, they don't. Most shippers go straight through Y-44 without ever stopping, and I hope that's what whoever put that bounty on our heads thinks we're gonna do. Besides, we're gonna be off again as soon as we can, hopefully before anybody picks up our trail."

I had to agree with his logic on that one. For once, his plan seemed solid to me.

"What about me?" Kell asked. "I can't just keep running forever. I've got a life too, you know."

"Well, we'll just have to, uh, figure that part out, I guess," he said from the cockpit in a subdued voice.

In my turret, I winced. I doubted the boss had thought that bit through yet, and I wasn't looking forward to him moping around after he had to say goodbye to the only girl who'd fallen for him since—well, I couldn't actually remember the last one, but it had been a long while.

We touched down in a cloud of brown dust, and the boss began shutting off systems. I did the same in the turret before climbing out to see Kell writing something on a scrap of paper as she sat on the couch. Curious, I took a step closer. When my shadow fell over her, she looked up, glared at me, and folded the paper over so I couldn't read it.

"Snake," my partner said as he squeezed out of the cockpit into the midships. "Don't bother with hooking up the utilities. We aren't here long enough to need them. Kell and I shouldn't be gone for more than an hour or so."

"Okay, fine. I should have the container opened by then, one way or another."

Kell frowned. "Are you sure that's a good idea? I really don't think we ought to do that."

"Uh, yeah, I'm sure," I said. "Whaddya want us to do, keep flying around carrying god knows what, waiting for random bounty hunters or whoever else to come blast our ass? No thanks."

"Snake's right, Kell. The longer we have it, the worse it is. But that's why we're checking the bounty on the net. That'll tell us what the real deal is, whether they're after us or just the cargo. Come on, let's go." The boss offered his hand to Kell, but she didn't take it.

"I have to go to the bathroom real quick," she said, pointing to the ship's tiny latrine. "I'll meet you out front."

He nodded and walked into the cargo bay. I followed.

"Boss," I said in a low voice so Kell couldn't hear. "Why is it every time we get close to finding out what's in there, she starts to get concerned? I'm telling you, there is something going on here, and your girl Kell knows what it is."

"There you go again, Snake," he replied with a sigh. "Did you not see her face when the bounty hunter tried to stamp us? She was terrified out of her fucking mind. And if she had anything to do with whoever put the bounty on us, why the hell would they be trying to kill us when she's onboard, huh?"

"Sure, she was scared, but I'm telling you, she knows more than she's telling. See if you can get it out of her. Pillow talk, you know?"

"You leave Kell to me, and you just get to work," he said.

"Fine," I said, rolling my eyes. As he walked down the ramp, I remembered I'd left my wallet with my cashcard in the midships storage locker. I turned around and walked back to the crew compartment.

Just as I stepped through the hatch, I met Kell. She looked over my shoulder, obviously checking to see where the boss was. When she saw he wasn't around, she leaned in close—real close—like breath-on-your-neck-cleavage-pressed-up-against-you close.

"Snake," she whispered in my ear, sending shivers of all types down my spine. "Don't open that container. It'll be better for all of us. You and me could be friends, Snake—close friends."

With that, she slid past me in the narrow hatch, emerald eyes flashing and hand brushing lightly across my chest as she made her way out. I watched her go, perfume trailing her in her form-fitting green dress.

Shit.

I'd normally be all about that series of events, except a) she was probably gonna get me killed; b) if she didn't get me killed and the boss found out, he'd probably kill me; and c) if the boss found out and he didn't kill me for some reason, the next time we ran into Carla, he'd probably let it slip and then she'd probably kill me. Or she might not—my relationship with Carla was hard to categorize, but since my kinda-sorta-maybe girlfriend was a dangerous bounty hunter and technically owned half the ship, it seemed best not to push my luck.

Kell gave me a warning look over her shoulder as she met my partner at the base of the ramp. He put his arm around her, and she leaned close against him as if there was nothing she wanted more. The look in the boss's eyes as they headed off together was one of pure bliss, but I hadn't felt more uneasy about things in a long time.

I needed to convince him that my instincts about Kell—as they were about most things having to do with women—were right, and his were wrong. The problem was, I didn't see Kell letting me get anywhere close to him without her being right there, especially not after that little stunt she'd just pulled.

But that would have to wait, because I had no intention of following Kell's instructions, enticing promises or not. I was going to get that damned container open.

I opened the locker and grabbed my wallet, then walked out into the bay, reached for a cigarette, and realized I'd left them in the turret. I shook my head, wondering if it was a lack of sleep that was getting to me, or my wariness of Kell, or whether my dull headache meant I'd hit my head harder going through that pickup truck window that I'd thought.

I went back amidships, dropped down in the turret, grabbed my smokes, and headed back out.

And right into trouble.

As I neared the end of the cargo bay, an unfamiliar man in dirty jeans and a dusty, faded burgundy T-shirt stepped onto the rear ramp. He took a worried glance over his shoulder and sprinted into the relative darkness of the ship. Backlit by San Pierre's bright sunlight, he was easy for me to see, but I must have been near invisible to him. I had just enough presence of mind to draw my knife from its sheath on the small of my back before he noticed me.

His mouth dropped open like they do in the movies when people are surprised, but before I could even warn him against it, his right hand reached for his leg holster. I managed to grab his gun hand with my left and brought my knife in for the kill with my right.

Or at least that's what was supposed to happen.

Instead, he saw the blade coming, grabbed my right hand at the wrist, and gave me a solid blow to the crotch with his knee. Meanwhile, he'd yanked his right hand free, which meant he could throw a sloppy haymaker at my face.

I ducked under the blow and grabbed his pistol.

He panicked, let go of my knife hand, and tried to keep me from getting his gun to avoid the eternal shame of being killed by his own pistol. Problem with his plan was, I didn't need a pistol to kill him. My E-14 combat knife would do just fine.

I aimed for his gut, but he was in the process of trying to knee me in the junk again, so instead I gave his upper thigh a stab all the way to the bone. He screamed like... well, like he'd just been stabbed, I guess.

I twisted the blade and yanked it back out.

He collapsed into the fetal position onto the deck, both hands around his leg and covered in blood. As he whimpered and writhed, I snatched the pistol out of his holster and kicked him in the ribs.

"Listen, motherfucker, what are you doing here? Saw the ramp down and thought nobody was around? Gonna sketch some shit right out from under my nose? You trying to take the ship or what?"

He moaned in response.

"Start talking, or else I'll open up your other leg."

"J-j-just trying to g-get the container," he said.

I looked into his wide, frightened eyes and scoffed. "Well, that seems to have been a pretty fucking bad idea, doesn't it? What'd you do, see two people leave and figure that was it? Did you really think we'd just leave the ship wide open so stupid shitstains like you could bebop on in here and sketch our stuff?"

"H-help me," he said. "I don't wanna die."

I snorted. "Seems like you shoulda thought about that *before* you came up in here looking to steal my shit and then pull a gun on me."

"I-I-I don't wanna die," he repeated, tears in his eyes.

"You're not gonna die, you stupid fuck. Not as long as you keep the pressure on that wound, anyway. Now, start talking. Who are you working for?"

"It's a bounty job," he whimpered.

"Yeah, I get that. I mean who put it out, and why are you the second guy I've met today who wants to blow up what-the-fuck-ever is in this stupid container?" I pointed with his pistol toward the source of our trouble.

"I-I-I don't wanna b-blow up anything," he rasped. "The bounty is for the c-container, unharmed."

Something wasn't adding up. The bounty hunter we'd tangled with before landing sure seemed to think he'd get paid by turning the container into pieces, so either one of the two fuckers trying to kill me didn't know how to read a bounty—which, while possible, seemed unlikely—or there was something else going on.

And whatever that something was, it made absolutely no sense to me.

"Okay, okay," I told the bleeding would-be cargo snatcher. "So let me get this straight, because you're making less sense than my fucking savings account. You're not here to blow anything up, just to snatch the container? Man, you *are* stupid. First off, you can't even move it. What were you gonna do, drag it out? The thing is fifteen meters long! And then you didn't even check to make sure the whole crew was gone? Always assume if something's too easy, you're not seeing the whole picture, dumbass."

"Ain't that the truth," an unfamiliar voice said.

I looked up to see a pair of goons at the base of the cargo ramp, pistols leveled in my direction.

Shit.

CHAPTER TEN

"Drop 'em," one of the goons said, nodding to my knife and recently acquired pistol.

I suppose the wise thing would have been to do what he said and try to talk my way out of it, but wisdom has never been one of my virtues.

I pulled the trigger three times as fast as I could while backpedaling toward the midships hatch and trying not to trip. The noise of the gunshots inside the bay's metal confines made my ears ring, as did the *snap snap snap* of rounds going past me and thudding into the bulkhead. I dove behind a large cardboard box that held a spare hydraulic pump I hoped would stop a bullet.

"Okay, boys," I shouted. "Let's talk about what's going on here, aight? I don't see any reason why—"

"You stabbed Quintin, you son of a bitch," one of them yelled back.

"Well, yeah," I said. "Your boy Quintin here pulled a gun on me, and if you fuckers were closer, maybe I'd stab you too. I mean, if I pulled a gun on you, you'd do the same, right? No harm, no foul. He'll live. Probably."

"You all right, Quintin?" one of the goons called.

"I-I think that—I dunno. I-i-it hurts so bad, man," Quintin said in shallows gasps from the floor.

I risked poking my head out from behind the box and noted with dismay that only one of my pursuers was visible, crouched low and far away, just outside the ship, barely leaning in enough to keep his pistol trained into the hold. Him I wasn't so worried about, but where was his partner? I ducked back down before he could pick me out in the darkened bay.

I heard someone moving from my right, on the other side of the mysterious cargo container everyone but me seemed to want. I glanced back over my shoulder at the midships hatch, now only a handful of meters away. If I made a run for it, I felt pretty confident the guy at the base of the ramp wouldn't be accurate enough to stamp me, but I couldn't be sure I could get the hatch closed before his buddy made it around the container to shoot me in the back.

"Listen to me," I shouted, keeping an eye on the far edge of the container where the second goon seemed likely to appear. "I'm gonna come out, but only if you promise to put the guns down, okay?"

"Yours first," came the reply from the foot of the cargo ramp.

"Okay, okay," I said. "I'm gonna stand up real slow, and I'm not gonna do anything crazy, okay?" I lied. I peeped my head around the box and saw the figure who had been outside creeping up the ramp, pistol high and at the ready. I knew the motherfucker planned on shooting me as soon as he saw me, and the only reason he wasn't shooting right now was that his eyes hadn't adjusted from the bright glare outside.

Exposing myself as little as I could, I took aim at his silhouette.

I got off one round before Quintin's cheap Glock knockoff stovepiped. *Fuck.*

Not only that, but I missed.

I leapt off the floor and threw the jammed pistol in the general direction of the now-retreating goon. For his part, he fired back wildly into the bay ceiling as he beat feet back down the ramp. While he ran away, I darted across the bay and planted my back firmly against the front of the shipping container, just underneath the strange, vented unit we'd noted during our first inspection of our trouble-causing cargo.

My ears rang and my heart thumped in my chest so loud it sounded like bass in a dance club. I unsheathed my knife and struggled to keep my breathing quiet as I waited for what I knew was coming next.

Sure enough, the third goon appeared from my left, probably expecting to find me still crouched behind my box farther away rather than just around the corner. Instead, I was almost on top of him.

I grabbed for his pistol with my left hand and stabbed hard and low with my right. My first strike sliced across the top of his arm before catching him in his right side. He had enough time to fire, deafening gunshots lighting up the cargo bay, before my second stab hit home. The goon gave a horrified scream, and his pistol clattered to the deck. He followed it to the floor, clutching his gut and trying to crawl away.

Wincing for the inevitable bullet to the back, I dashed across the bay through the midships hatch, where I hit the bay door switch to close it, then flipped the manual release to lock it from the inside. A pair of loud pings against the hatch told me the goon at the base of the ramp was back at it.

I swore and slipped into the cockpit, squinting at San Pierre's blinding sun shining in through the forward windshield. I opened the cockpit hatch that the boss rarely used, then dropped a meter to the dust by the forward landing gear. I surveyed the spaceport, shielding my eyes from the sun as I tried to figure out if there was anybody else around waiting to come kill me. To my relief, the spaceport wasn't very busy, and if anyone noticed the gun battle that had occurred inside our Black Sun, they didn't seem to care. Nobody even gave me a second glance as I sneaked down the starboard side of the ship, sticking close to the hull in case the other goon decided to come back outside and look forward.

When I crept around the rear landing skids and onto the cargo ramp, I saw the final thug, his pistol up and back to me, staring into the bay.

"Jake? You all right?" he called. "If you can hear me, buddy, just say something, okay?"

There was a moan in response.

"Quintin, can you see Jake? Or that motherfucker?"

"N-no, I can't s-see shit, man. I'm hurt bad," Quintin gasped.

I slipped up behind the goon and put my knife to his throat, trying to keep my hands as steady as I could, given the adrenaline pumping through me like a hot batch of Z.

"Don't fucking move," I said

Of course, he didn't listen.

He tried to spin away and bring his pistol to bear on me. All he got for his trouble was a shallow slice across his neck, followed by a much deeper one across his chest as I struggled to keep him close and under control. If my younger days had taught me anything, it was that the guy with the knife either stayed close enough to his enemies to fuck them, or *he'd* be the one getting fucked.

He screamed and smashed me in the side of the face with his pistol. I saw stars. I swung my knife blindly in a low arc, and it caught his jeans and tugged a ragged cut from his left hip up to his stomach.

He stumbled back into the bay, firing once. The shot went wide into the spaceport maintenance shops behind me as I turned to run.

I lost my footing and tripped on the ramp, falling backward and landing hard enough for it to knock the wind out of me. I rolled off the side of the ramp into the dust, scrambled to my feet, and punched in the five-digit code to close the bay door.

I'd never been so relieved to hear the sound of that aft hydraulic pump struggling to do its job. When the bay closed, I flipped the safety lever to external lock and listened for the metallic snick of the safety bolts. Only then did I sit down in the shade of the ship and lean back against the aft rear landing skid, my head and heart pounding, ears ringing, and hands shaking.

I lit a cigarette and felt for my wallet.

I needed a drink.

CHAPTER ELEVEN

The boss and Kell showed up about fifteen minutes later.

He did not seem thrilled to find me reclined in the shadow of the ship with a fifth of cheap scotch in my hand and a pile of cigarette butts beside me.

"What the fuck are you doing drinking Scotch in the middle of the afternoon?" he asked.

"It's what they had. I asked for bourbon, but they were out."

His expression darkened. "You know what I mean, Snake. You were supposed to get the goddamn container open! Kell and I practically ran all the way over there and all the way back, looking over our shoulders the whole fucking time, and you're just chilling here drinking? What the fuck is wrong with you?"

I snorted. "First off, I've only gotten to enjoy a couple of pulls, and do you know why? Because as soon as you left, I got jumped by three motherfuckers trying to jack Kell's precious cargo here and—"

"It's not mine!" she said, eyes blazing.

"Whatever." I gave her a dismissive wave. "Bottom line is, three dudes came up in here, armed to the teeth and ready to rumble, and next thing I know it's a fucking war movie in there." I nodded to the ship. "I'm pretty damn lucky to still be alive, so I figured I deserved a drink."

"So where are they?" the boss answered, glancing around the spaceport.

"They're still in there. I locked the midships from the inside and then locked the cargo door from outside."

"What? Are they still alive?"

"I dunno. Maybe."

"Well, did you get one of their guns or something? Did you shoot any of them?"

"Nope. But I stabbed all of 'em. Pretty bad, too, I think."

Kell looked like she wanted to throw up.

"So, you mean to tell me that when we open this door, there's either gonna be a buncha bodies or some dudes with guns who are mad as hornets and ready to shoot their way out?" the boss asked.

"Yep."

"Jesus Christ, Snake. Can I not leave you alone for half an hour?"

I shrugged. "Next time, you stay and handle it then."

He sighed and turned to Kell. "All right, Kell, stay back. I'm gonna open this thing up and—"

"Whoa, whoa," I interrupted. "Let's be smart about this. I say we take off, depressurize the hold, wait a minute or two to make sure all of 'em's dead, repressurize, then clean up the mess."

"No way," he said. "I'm not taking off with three guys in the hold with guns. They could damage a lot of shit back there. Maybe they already have. Hell, if they know what they're doing, they can get into the maintenance access and we'll all be fucked. We deal with them down here."

I scowled. He had a point.

"Fine," I muttered. "But I don't have a gun, and I think I've done more than my fair share. So, I'll open the door and you be ready. And you'd better shoot straighter than you normally do."

Kell moved away from the entrance while I unlatched the door safety and the boss took up a good, two-handed pistol stance facing the bay door.

I punched in the code and the ramp slowly descended.

The dark bay was silent.

I could barely make out Quintin's body where he'd lain before, and thought I saw someone else nearby.

"Snake, lights," the boss said, not lowering his pistol.

I muttered a curse and stole up the ramp, flipping the bank of master switches on the port side. The bay lights flickered to life. I heard Kell retch into the San Pierre dust.

The place looked like a horror movie. Quintin had apparently succumbed to his wounds, but not before he'd bled all over the deck, and the last guy I'd cut had decided to collapse and bleed out a meter away from him, just in front of the cargo container, but there was blood all over the place from where he'd tried to find something to bind his wounds in the dark.

"Didn't you say there were three of them?" the boss asked.

"Yeah. I think the other one's up front."

We walked forward until we found his body, in a pool of blood at the far end of the bay.

My partner rolled him over with his foot, grimacing at the extent of the man's stomach wounds.

"Jesus, Snake."

I shrugged. "I didn't start it."

"You need to get a gun."

"Why? You think it's any better dying getting shot than it is getting stabbed?"

"No, it's just—"

"Never mind that," I whispered, taking advantage of the fact that Kell wasn't around. "Listen. Kell is trouble, man, she tried to—"

"Snake, we're not having this discussion when—"

"Uh, guys," I heard Kell say from the other end of the bay. "The cops are here."

"Shit," my partner muttered.

He holstered his pistol and we walked back toward the rear hatch, where a pair of San Pierre's finest waited for us, sporting shotguns and black body armor.

"How can I help you, gentlemen?" the boss asked in his cheeriest nothing-to-see-here voice.

"We got reports that there may have been some kind of violence going on onboard. Witnesses reported gunshots. We just wanted to check in and make sure everything was okay before we bothered making a report. We'd hate to make something out of nothing," one of the cops said.

My partner sighed and withdrew his wallet.

"No need for any kind of report, officer, because there was no violence," I said. "Just some maintenance issues. Hydraulic problems. They probably just heard one of the valves bust."

The boss handed over a pair of brown, hundred-credit notes to the speaking cop.

"Uh-huh," the other cop said. "And what about that?" He pointed to my chest. "It sure looks like you got up to some trouble."

I looked down and realized my T-shirt and jeans were spattered with blood.

I shrugged. "That's nothing. Cut myself shaving this morning."

The boss handed over another pair of bills.

"And them?" the first cop said, pointing a finger at the two dead bodies visible from the bay's entrance.

"Oh, you mean Bo and Luke there?" the boss asked. "They're just good ole boys, never meaning no harm. They're resting. Tired from a long flight." He pulled out a pair of green five-hundred credit notes and handed one to each cop.

The cops smiled and nodded. "Well, sorry to have bothered you two over nothing. Have a good day."

"You too, officers," the boss said with a smile.

The smile left as soon as they walked away. "God, I hate cops."

"Well, coulda been worse," I said. "They could've actually arrested me. Granted, I'd get let go eventually, but by then, every hunter in the quadrant would be on us like flies on shit."

"Yeah," Kell said with a shiver as she leaned against the boss. "Let's get out of here before that happens. I don't think we should stick around."

"Yeah, I guess not," the boss agreed. "But I still wanna know what it is we got back there."

"Why? I say we just leave it here," I said, ignoring the fire in Kell's eyes.

"I don't think that's gonna work, Snake," he said. "The bounty news isn't good, man. There's two competing bounties. One for the cargo intact, and one for it destroyed. The one with the cargo intact also has a rider bounty for the party that destroys it."

My head swam. Why did this shit always seem to happen to us?

"So, we have two bounties on us? What the fuck kind of sense does that make? One of them would just—"

"The payout keeps changing. Both parties are trying to outbid each other," the boss said.

"Never felt more valued in my life," I muttered.

"Yeah," he agreed. "So, let's just hose the cargo bay out from your little adventure back there and get outta here."

"And the bodies?"

"Put 'em in a box, I guess, and we'll leave 'em here."

I lit another cigarette. "Gotta love this job."

He turned to Kell. "You all right, baby?"

"Yeah, I think so," she said. "It's just a little shocking to me—I mean, all this violence and blood. I've never—I've never really been around this kind of thing, that's all."

"Well, now's your chance to check that off the bucket list," I said. "Give me a hand cleaning out the bay and it'll never bother you again."

Kell blanched and the boss gave me a warning look. I sighed and went to get a hose.

———————

We rocketed off the surface half an hour later with no agreed-on destination except for someplace that wasn't San Pierre.

"I'm telling you, boss, we gotta make a break for someplace bigger. If we got two bounties out on us, we gotta get someplace we can hide in the crowd," I said from the turret as I scanned the traffic around San Pierre.

"I agree we need to hide, but that's why going someplace bigger is the exact opposite of what we should do," the boss said from the cockpit. "The more people there are, the more eyes and ears. Hunters may usually work alone, but you know as well as I do that they'll pay for scraps of info, and I don't like the idea of having to worry every eyeball that sees me is gonna sell me out for a coupla thou off the top of the contract."

"What about someplace out of the way like Ottawa Station?" Kell asked.

"You call that out of the way?" I said with a snort. "That's four jumps from Sol. It's practically the Inner Ring. We might as well go to Mars. That's where the big fish swim. No thanks."

"Yeah," the boss agreed from the cockpit. "We gotta get farther out, but we're gonna have to be careful getting there. From here we've only got jumps back to Yaeger, the T-12, and Ju-Ho. I guarantee they'll be waiting for us back at Yaeger and—"

"Can't do Ju-Ho either, boss. Don't Oxford Don and his crew work out of Uyu Dosi? Isn't that in Ju-Ho?"

"Shit. Yeah, it is. I guess we hit the T-12 and from there to Guten Hafen. Maybe hide out at Farhold until we can figure shit out. If shit gets too tough, I guess we could duck into the DuLalle Republic."

"DuLalle? That's… non-federated space, right?" Kell asked, worry in her voice. "I didn't think bounty hunters had to announce or anything out there. I heard they can just kill you without warning out there, since the UNF doesn't have jurisdiction."

"Yeah, but they do that half the time anyway," I pointed out. "And DuLalle's pretty well policed— it's just not in the UNF. Yet."

"Yo, Snake, we got a voicemail. It's from Jade's account."

Which meant it was really from Carla. My ears perked up.

"Yeah, when did it come in?"

"While we were patched into the net down on San Pierre. I just didn't see it until now. She sent it three hours ago. The message title says, 'This is for the both of you.'"

"Who is Jade?" Kell asked.

"A friend of Carla, who is Snake's… girlfriend or whatever. Carla says she's not on the net, which seems insane, but she doesn't seem to have an account or a logon ID, so everything we ever get from her comes from Jade."

"Well, play the damn thing," I said from my turret.

The ship's computer beeped and Carla's voice came over the comms. The dull hum of a life support system and a soft warning chime in the background told me she had recorded the message from her cockpit.

"What the fuck have you two gotten yourselves into? The hottest ticket out there right now is for a pair of schmucks in a beat-up Black Sun 490, last seen on Yaeger in the company of a red-haired woman, carrying a hot cargo that somebody wants blown up in the worst of ways and that somebody else desperately doesn't want anything to happen to. I don't know who the girl is, but I know the other two have to be you, because this sounds exactly like the kind of shitstorm you two would find your way into."

Of all the people I've ever met, Carla is the one who gets me the most.

"I don't know where you are exactly, but I'd bet you're not far from Yaeger. San Pierre, probably. Anyway, if you get this message and you're there, don't head back to Yaeger, and don't go through the T-12 either. A pair of guys I know working for BlueSpear are hanging out there waiting for you, and there's enough firepower headed to Yaeger right now to turn your flying scrap heap into a solid chunk of metal. I know you'd normally stay out of Ju-Ho on account of Oxford Don, but I got a reliable source that says his crew is working something in Mite's Point right now. That's your best shot. Get to Ju-Ho, lay low, and I'll try to meet you on Meridian in two days. If I'm wrong, and it isn't you, drop a line to Jade and let me know. I got bounties to pursue and shit to do besides look after you two."

The ship heeled to starboard and the autopilot chimed.

"Wait, we're going to listen to her?" Kell asked. "Didn't she say something about bounties? What makes you think she won't just jump you and claim the bounty herself?"

"Nah," I said. "Carla's not that way. There are some loyal people out there, you know." I stood halfway out of the turret to make eye contact with Kell. Her eyes met mine but betrayed nothing.

"Snake's right," the boss agreed. "Carla's not gonna pull a fast one on us. She's had plenty of chances to screw us and she hasn't yet so—"

"Oh, she's screwed one of us," I said with a grin.

"Shut up, Snake. You know what I mean."

"Besides, she owns half the ship," I pointed out. "So, we kinda have to listen to her."

"You said Snake owned half the ship," Kell said to the boss.

"It's a long story."

The boss set the radar to audibly warn us whenever anybody got within 250k and let himself out of the cockpit to plop down on the couch next to Kell.

Above my head, I slid the turret maglock hatch closed, sealing the turret off from the midships. It was six hours to the Ju-Ho jump point, and I had no desire to know what those two were up to. Besides, the long hours since I'd slept last had caught up to me. I put in a pair of headphones, took a long pull off my bottle of scotch, and went to sleep.

CHAPTER TWELVE

I woke with the overwhelming need to piss. I looked at my watch. We still had an hour and some change left until the jump point. I took out my headphones and put my ear to the turret maglock. I didn't hear any obvious sounds of sexual activity, so I opened the maglock and poked my head out.

The boss and Kell lay on the couch under one of the foil-lined emergency blankets from the ship's evac kit. They both looked sound enough asleep, so I climbed out of the turret as silently as I could and made my way past them to the cramped latrine closet.

Once I finished my business, I slipped through the open midships hatch out into the cargo bay. The mysterious container sat there, mocking me with the fact that whatever was inside was probably going to get me killed and I wasn't even going to know why. I wondered if the boss would lose his mind if I went back to the crew compartment, closed the internal hatch, and then vented the cargo bay out into space.

Sure, we had the tractor beam, but I doubted it was powerful enough to move anything near the size of a standard shipping container. I chuckled, imagining Kell's face when she woke up to me having ruined her grand plans. I about jumped out of my skin when I turned around to find her standing in the hatch, watching me.

She wore a T-shirt that barely reached her upper thighs and nothing else. She brushed her hair out of her eyes as I looked her over.

"Whatcha up to, Snake?" she asked, as if it were the most natural thing in the world.

"I was just thinking about venting this fucking box of trouble out into the void, that's all."

She frowned. "You don't want to do that."

"Oh, but I do. See, I dunno if you've noticed, but people keep trying to kill us over whatever's in here, so I'd just as soon be clear of it."

She shook her head and smiled, stepping into the bay with me.

"C'mon, Snake. Remember what I said. You just help me make sure he leaves this thing alone and we can be friends." She took another step closer and put her hand on my chest. She looked up at me with dazzling eyes, then bit her bottom lip and winked. I had to admit, she was damn good at being the bad girl.

"Look, Kell, I think you got the wrong idea about me."

"Do I?"

"Yeah. See, I may not be a—"

"You're a man, Snake. And I know men."

"I'm sure you do. You certainly know my partner in there, don't you? You got him wrapped around your pretty little finger. And that's fine, for as long as it lasts. But I think you're reading me wrong. Sure, I'm just a lowdown dirty ex-con with a thing for pretty girls, booze, and violence. There's a reason I got the nickname Snake, after all. But here's the thing, Kell. I may be a snake, but I ain't a goddamn rat bastard. And I'd have to be a rat bastard to fuck my boy's girl on his ship, right under his nose, and while he thinks he's sleeping next to her—I mean any one or two of those, sure, but not all three. So come off it. Plus, it kinda ruins the thrill, since I know that you're just trying to use me to keep control of whatever's in there." I pointed to the container. "You might have better luck if you just came clean with me and told me what the fuck is going on."

"You wouldn't understand."

"Try me," I said.

She shook her head.

"Well then, you just know this, Kell. You think you can control him, but I know him better than you do, and I'll just tell—"

"I told him you kept eyeing me and that you hit on me when he wasn't looking. And I told him you would probably tell some crazy lies about me because I'd rejected you." She gave me a triumphant smile.

"You evil bitch," I said, eyes wide. "You really are fucking evil, and I don't say that very often. You know neither one of us has a lot of friends, right?"

She shrugged. "He's got me."

My mouth dropped open at her audacity. This girl was both crazy dangerous and dangerously crazy. They don't come around like that very often. I seriously considered choking the shit out of her right there in the cargo bay.

"Leave the container where it is until I say otherwise, got it?" she said, her earlier seductiveness replaced with cold malice. She turned around and went back into the midships.

"Watch your back, Kell," I muttered.

She turned around and gave me a devilish smile that made me shiver. "And you watch yours."

CHAPTER THIRTEEN

I sat in the turret, stomach churning. We'd made it through the Ju-Ho jump point without trouble, and the nav lane on the other side was empty, but that didn't make me feel better. I cast a nervous glance up at the open turret hatch above me as the boss and Kell kept up a cheerful patter of conversation. I didn't know if the fatal blow was going to be a missile from some bounty hunter Carla didn't know had moved into Ju-Ho during Oxford Don's absence or from the devil-with-a-killer-bod that called herself Kell, but I could feel it coming.

"Yo, Snake, you're being awful quiet down there," the boss said from the cockpit. "What's up?"

"Nothing much. Just trying to keep a good watch out." *Although the most dangerous thing in the whole damn sector is sitting on the couch right above me,* I didn't add.

"Must be rough on you, seeing me with Kell," the boss said. My blood ran cold. "But now you know how I feel every time you and Carla get together and I just wind up staying onboard and updating the navigation software." He laughed.

"Heh. Yeah," I said with as much humor as I could muster. "And being you is no fun."

"Har har."

"Hey, boss, how much longer until we make Meridian anyway?" I asked, hoping to steer the conversation away from anything to do with Kell or their relationship.

"Uhh, looks like about fifteen hours, I think. You ever been there?"

"Nope."

"Yeah, me neither. What about you, Kell?" he asked.

"Nuh-uh. I don't even think I've ever been to Ju-Ho before."

"Yeah, it's not exactly a bustling center of commerce."

"Well, I hope Carla's right and we can lay low there," I said. "After our trouble around San Pierre, I can live with a little peace and quiet where nobody's looking to hull us or shoot me."

"I bet this whole thing blows over in about a week anyway," Kell mused.

Something about the way she said it made my eyes narrow. "What's that supposed to mean?" I asked.

"Nothing. It's not supposed to mean anything."

The boss chuckled. "Oh, that we could be so lucky. I don't think you understand how these things work, Kell. They don't exactly just 'blow over.' If you're gonna go through the trouble of putting a bounty—and a sizeable one at that—on somebody or something, you don't usually set an expiration date."

"That reminds me of something I forgot to ask," I said. "How much was the bounty anyway, when you guys checked at San Pierre?"

"At the time, the destroy bounty was at 75.5k. The 'return unharmed' bounty was at 82k. Plus a 20k rider on whoever was responsible for destroying the container, if somebody chose to execute the other bounty. But when you looked at the history, it had gone back and forth. Whoever's putting those bounties out has some pretty deep pockets."

I rubbed my face. That was a lot of money. I'd heard of higher price tags for sure, but those numbers still put the price on our heads higher than probably seventy-five percent of the contracts on the market.

"You know, part of me wants to know what the hell is going on, but the other part of me thinks the less I know, the better, you know? An ignorance-is-bliss kind of thing," I mused.

"That's probably the smartest way to think about it," Kell said in a knowing tone. "Sometimes it's best just to let things go."

In my turret, I allowed myself a wry smile.

That's right, bitch, you just keep thinking I'm done looking into whatever it is you've got going on. Don't you worry your pretty little head about Snake anymore.

We'll see who gets bitten.

"Yo, Snake, I got a kilo class power sig coming up on our tail from the jump point. You tracking him? He's still a ways out, but he's closing fast."

My smile disappeared.

I checked the radar and swore. I couldn't see thermal signatures or engine outputs at my station, but the lone blip on the scope was definitely getting closer. I slewed the turret around and zoomed in with my gun camera. A far speck of light resolved into a fast-moving red fighter, backlit by the glow of his afterburners.

"Yeah, boss, I see him. Single ship. Fighter—Mitsubishi, but hard to tell which model. Javelin or a Blazewing, maybe? He's still way too far out to worry about, but if he keeps up his current course and speed, he's gonna get to us long before we get to Meridian."

"Fuck."

"Yeah. Whatcha think? All power to engines and make a break for it?"

"Nah. Won't do any good. He'd still catch us, even at full burners. It'd just take him a bit longer. Plus, if we increase speed to run, he'll know for sure he's got the right Black Sun. We're just gonna play it cool for the time being."

I digested that for a moment before I answered. "Playing it cool ain't usually our strong suit, boss."

"Yeah, I know. But when I say, 'play it cool,' I really mean 'pretend we're not worried about him so we can lure him in close enough to blast his ass into little pieces.' That better?"

"Much."

I kept him in my sights the next three hours, but he slowed as he drew closer, eventually settling into a trailing position at six low and about a thousand klicks out—too far for guns and missiles, but close enough to where he could get in range in a minute or two if he chose to. He stayed off comms, never scanned us or even switched on a targeting radar, but didn't leave us either. I kept on edge for the next twelve hours, waiting for him to make a move, but he never did.

By the time the nav computer chimed with an incoming message from Meridian's automated landing system and the boss announced we had clearance to land, my eyes stung, my head throbbed, my joints hurt from staying in the turret the whole time, and my fingers ached. I was completely spent.

"Man, fuck that asshole," I growled. "This stupid son of a bitch has had me watching him for fifteen fucking hours straight and he hasn't so much as twitched a finger in our direction. You know what? I don't care if he was originally coming after us or not—I hope he does now, just because I want to fuck him up."

"You have anger management problems, Snake," Kell said from close above me.

I looked up to see her peering down at me from the turret ring. "You think so? You ought to keep that in mind," I muttered.

"No, you ought to keep it in mind, because when people get angry, they do stupid things, and that doesn't benefit anybody."

We began our descent into Meridian's atmosphere, but the red Mitsubishi didn't follow, at least not immediately. As we lost him in the haze of the upper atmosphere, I shook my head. Again, I got the feeling there was something going on I wasn't privy to. It had become a far-too-familiar feeling in the past couple of days.

I took my eyes off the fighter to glare at Kell. "I keep getting the feeling you're trying to tell me something, but you're being all vague and shit about it. So, if you got something to say to me, fucking say it."

"Fine," she whispered, leaning down into the turret. "Here it is, then, for the last time: stay out of my way."

CHAPTER FOURTEEN

The spaceport in Meridian turned out to be located amid rolling, grass-covered hills, next to a broad, shallow river. There wasn't much of a city around it, just a bar or two, a single run-down motel, the usual handful of customs and legal offices, and a pair of maintenance shops that looked like they'd seen better days. The only other ship on the pad was an ancient Ford-Tata Hercules that looked like it hadn't lifted off since God was a kid. I could see why Carla picked this as a place for us to hide out.

Why would anybody bother chasing somebody down on Meridian to kill them, when it was likely boredom would do the job just as well?

The boss powered the engines down, dropped the ramp, and climbed out of the cockpit.

"Damn," he said, running a hand across his weary face. "What a run. Let's get hooked up to the utilities and get ourselves something to eat. These energy bars are killing me. Why do you always get banana anyway, Snake?"

"When you send me to buy 'em, you get what I pick out," I said as I stood out of the turret, stretching my tired muscles.

"What about you?" the boss said to Kell. "How you doing?"

"Same as you two. Ready to be off the ship for a bit and looking forward to some real food. And maybe something to drink."

"That is a good idea," he said.

"I hate to remind you, but there's still a teeny problem." I pointed to the cargo bay. "Let's not forget about the box of bad vibes in the hold, okay? I'm not letting my guard down until we know what the fuck is going on with it and then get rid of it. Like the rest of the trash."

I flicked my gaze to Kell, but she ignored me.

"There's nobody down here but us," the boss said. "But I agree, somebody's got to stay and watch it, and that—"

"How about you stay on guard tonight, Snake, and we'll go out and bring you something back, and then tomorrow, since Carla or whatever her name is will be here, you can go out and we'll hold things down here," Kell offered with a sincerity that made me nauseous.

"No. That's not a—"

"Seems like a good idea to me. We'll go get some rest in the motel tonight and then you can go tomorrow," the boss interrupted, a gleam in his eye. I knew what he had in mind, and while it involved the motel, it sure as hell didn't involve any rest.

I shook my head. "Seriously, we're not out of this shit yet, whatever 'this shit' is, and we need to—"

"Don't worry about everything so much, Snake. Besides, you'll have plenty of time to get those locks open and find out what it is everybody's after by the time Carla gets here."

Kell's mouth tightened, and she gave me an almost imperceptible shake of her head.

I smiled a wide, triumphant smile as if it were the best thing I'd heard in a long time. "You know, bossman, when you put it like that, maybe it is a good idea for you two to head out. I'm sure I'll get plenty of work done while you're gone."

"I thought you said you weren't going to open the container," Kell told the boss.

"I did, but I just meant on San Pierre after we got jumped because I was worried another crew would come after us. Here, we got the time and I know there won't be anybody else using the tools, so we may as well crack it open. That's the key to this whole mess, really. We gotta find out what the hell it is everybody wants so badly."

"But what if—"

"Kell, seriously, listen," he said. "There's no danger in opening that thing up. I know you're worried about the bounty rider if it gets destroyed, but I'm telling you, nobody is going to come after you. You're just somebody who got rolled into this. 'Wrong place, wrong time' kinda thing, you know?"

I could barely keep the smile off my face.

How you gonna beat the game this time, bitch?

———————————————

While I connected the ship to spaceport power and water, Kell freshened up inside, chatting with the boss the whole time—to make sure I didn't have a chance to talk to him, no doubt. After I verified the utility connections, I trudged across the concrete pad to the closest maintenance shop. There I rented out a plasma cutter, a cold snip set with its associated cryo tanks, and a slag blanket. I paid and got the clerk to throw all of it in the back of the shop's pickup and drive me back to the ship.

By the time I got there, the boss and Kell were already gone, and the ship locked up. I unloaded the truck, typed in the code to open the cargo bay, lit a cigarette, and set to work. When I plugged the plasma cutter into the high-voltage plug, it tripped the number four circuit breaker, so I went back into the crew compartment to reset it.

Just as I turned around to head back into the cargo bay, I noticed an unfamiliar scrap of blue paper in the cockpit, sitting atop the well-worn Black Sun preflight manual. The sheet had the boss's name in a feminine script that could only be Kell's. I glanced over my shoulder to make sure I was alone, and being the kind of guy I am, unfolded the letter and read it. The note inside was in the same handwriting, although it looked as though she'd rushed to finish it.

You're probably going to hate me forever, but just understand I didn't want it to get this far, and when I first sat down to talk to you in that bar on Yaeger I never thought it would end up like it has. Nobody was ever supposed to get hurt too much. Please, please, believe me. I really mean it. Still, I enjoyed our time together for the most part, and the whole thing isn't as bad as it seems. I promise it's more complicated than you know. I really didn't want it to turn out this way and I hope no one else gets hurt, but I promise tonight was for the best. It's just business, in the end.

If you ever get out to Ottawa Station, swing by the Hilcolmb Building and ask for me. Somebody there will know how to find me, and we'll go out and get a drink and laugh about all this.

Love,

Kell

PS: Don't bring Snake.

I shook my head as I folded the letter up and put it in my pocket.

That seductive, conniving, scheming, lying bitch was not only going to get us killed, but she was going to do the one fucking thing I'd told her I was worried about and break the boss's heart.

I sighed.

He sure knew how to pick 'em.

I thought about trying to find the boss and warn him but figured it was a lot of effort and wouldn't change anything anyway. I shrugged, went back into the bay, plugged the plasma cutter back in, and began setting up the cold snips. While the cryo tanks cycled, I smoked another cigarette and thought things over.

The way I saw it, the note meant she didn't think she'd be coming back to the ship. If that was her plan, I expected her to make it a quick break with the boss so she could be off to the next phase of whatever scheme she was up to. I had the sudden thought that perhaps the red Mitsubishi was one of her companions, just waiting for her signal—the only question was, signal for what?

The control panel on the cryo tank beeped, telling me the cold snip system was ready. I stamped out my cigarette and pulled on the safety gloves. Just as I was about to get started, truck tires sounded on the concrete, and I heard a pair of doors open and shut.

I swore as I watched the bottom of the ramp in disbelief, half expecting to get attacked in the bay by yet another set of bounty hunters.

Instead, Kell climbed up the ramp first, her clutch purse in her hand, rushing past me toward the midships. The boss followed her a few seconds later, taking off his shoulder holster and hanging it on the hook in the cargo bay as he walked past.

The puzzled look must have shown on my face. "What?" he asked.

"What are you two doing back?"

He shrugged. "I decided I needed to get a different shirt before we went out. I noticed this one has blood on it from when we cleared the bay back on San Pierre." He pointed to a spot of blood on his shirt that I couldn't see.

"Uh, okay, man. Sure."

He slipped past Kell as she exited the midships and he made his way inside. She made a beeline for me, a look of barely controlled fury in her eyes.

"Been busy getting into other people's business?" she hissed, not bothering to hide the malice in her voice.

I took off the safety gloves and lit a cigarette before I answered.

"I dunno what you're talking about. I've just been getting ready to open this thing up. It's gonna be a lot of work. But it would just bore you, seeing as how you already know what's in here anyway, don't you?" I held up my hand. "But don't tell me, though. I like surprises. So, you two go on out and have a good time, and you can see it when you get back tomorrow." I smiled a sharkish grin. "You are planning on coming back, aren't you, Kell?"

"*You,*" she seethed.

"What?"

"You know what."

"What's the matter? Did you go in there looking to grab something before our 'mutual friend' could find it? Don't worry, I got it for you." I patted the jeans pocket that held her note.

"You—"

I put my finger in her face, and her mouth snapped shut. "Listen, you piece of shit. You got two choices. First choice is you walk your pretty, conniving ass right down that fucking ramp, hop into that truck, drive away, and hope to god we never run across you again—and I'm only giving you that option because he's fond of you, not because I am, so don't get it twisted. The second option is that you stay right here and when he comes back out, I'm gonna read him this fucking letter and you're gonna tell us what the hell is going on. Your choice."

The boss reemerged from the midships in a new shirt. "Hey, Kell, you ready to go?" he asked from the far end of the bay.

"Actually, Kell's got a little something she'd like to tell you," I said, reaching for her arm.

Kell's face twisted into a mask of fury as she spun out of my grasp.

The brief second it took me to realize what she was doing was a second too long.

She snatched my partner's .45 revolver out of where it hung in his holster on the wall and pointed it straight at my face from just over a meter away. At that range, a blind, quadriplegic monkey with polio couldn't miss.

My heart skipped a beat, and I have to admit the only thought that ran through my head was *I am going to be so fucking pissed if his pistol is what kills me.*

I put my hands up as I tried to back away, but she had me backed up flat against the cargo container.

"Whoa there, Kell," I said. "Let's not get—"

"Save it, Snake. I'm not the one that made this happen. You did. If you'd have listened to me, everything would be fine."

"Kell, what are you doing?" the boss said, confusion in his voice. He took a step toward her.

The pistol swung to him, but he didn't stop walking.

"Stay where you are or I'll do it," Kell warned. He froze.

I started to put a hand down so I could get my knife, but Kell snapped the pistol back to me.

"Don't even think about it, Snake. Pull that blade out—slowly." I did as she instructed and started to bend to put it on the deck. "Nooo, Snake. None of that. Throw it away, over there." She flicked the barrel toward the ramp, and I tossed my E-14 outside.

"Kell," the boss said. "Don't do this. Just don't." He began walking toward her again.

"I'm warning you," she shouted, taking a step closer to me and keeping the massive barrel of the pistol between my eyes. "I will kill him! I will! I like you, but him I don't give a fuck about."

My mind raced almost as fast as my heart while I tried to come up with an ending to this situation that didn't involve my brain matter splattered all across the cargo bay.

"Bossman, I think—uh—I think she's serious. So, let's just not push things, okay?"

"I got this, Snake," he said as he took another step toward her. "I know Kell better than you do, and I know she's not gonna hurt you."

Oh fuck.

"Boss, believe me when I tell you '*no you fucking don't,*' so just chill with the walking toward her, okay?"

"Kell, listen to me," he said soothingly. "You don't want to do this. I don't know what's going on, but I promise we can work it out." By now, he was almost on top of her, hands outspread and pleading. She pointed the pistol at his chest.

Her finger tightened on the trigger, and I winced, waiting for the shot and desperately hoping for some sort of miracle where he didn't take a .45 round clean through the heart and bleed to death on the deck.

Instead, before my brain could even form a coherent, panicked shout, she swung the barrel around to me and pulled the trigger.

CHAPTER FIFTEEN

The hammer fell with a harmless click.

I almost fainted.

I watched, dumbfounded, as she squeezed the trigger again. *Click.* She took a step back, pointed the pistol at the boss, and squeezed the trigger again—*click*.

The boss folded his arms in front of him and sighed.

"Are we done yet, Kell? No matter how many times you pull it, you aren't gonna shoot anybody. The bullets are in my pocket. I left my pistol there for you because I wanted to see what you'd do when you saw Snake was finally gonna open up the container."

My mouth dropped open. Of all the stupid, cheesy, only-in-the-movies, Hollywood-holo bullshit cliches in the world, my boss—this motherfucker right here—had actually gotten the old "unload the gun to flush out the traitor" trick to work?

Holy fucking shit.

Kell looked as dumbfounded as I did.

Unfortunately, that only lasted for an eyeblink before she pistol-whipped him right in the face and sent him staggering backward clutching a bloody nose.

I guess that's why they only do that trick in the movies.

I leapt at her, but she sidestepped me, bashed me in the side of my head with the pistol, and stuck out her foot to trip me. My head throbbed and vision flashed white as I crashed hard into the bay's opposite wall. I heard a footstep behind me, and I only just got an arm up before she brought the gun barrel down again.

I deflected the blow, swung at her and missed, but was able to grab the pistol with my other hand, wrenching it from her grasp and sending it clattering to the deck.

She backpedaled, reaching inside her purse.

I darted toward her and immediately regretted it.

Her hand emerged, clutching what I recognized as a two-shot Yang Arms .32 Hidden Stinger. I dove out of the way, landing hard on a toolbox and scattering screwdrivers and wrenches across the bay. She fired twice, the first round pinging off the deck behind me and the second one making a metallic splat as it impacted the rear bulkhead.

She fled down the cargo ramp as I staggered to my feet, nursing my pounding head and a twisted ankle. The truck door slammed and tires squealed.

Kell was gone.

The boss groaned as he sat up, trying and failing to stem the rush of blood from his nose with his right hand. I sat down and closed my eyes, fighting back waves of throbbing nausea and trying to stay conscious.

"Well, shit," I muttered.

"I fink shthe broke mah fuhthkin nothe," he said.

"Yeah, that's probably a safe bet."

"Fuhk."

A quick set, a shot of Iostican, some gauze, two slugs of scotch, and thirty minutes later, the boss's nose had finally quit bleeding and returned to near its normal size.

We sat on the cargo bay deck, backs against the shipping container, as I lit a cigarette and he passed the bottle of scotch to me. I took a swig and sighed.

"So, you ready to explain all that shit back there or what?" I asked.

"Whaddya mean?"

"I mean the whole 'unload the gun without telling me' bullshit. That's what I mean."

He shrugged. "Seemed like a good idea at the time. I was pretty sure something was up, but I didn't want to ruin stuff with Kell if I was wrong."

"And what clued you in? The fact that we kept getting jumped or the fact that she'd have done anything to keep us from opening this fucking box?"

"Actually, what clued me in was she gave me some bullshit about you coming onto her and being pissed when she rejected you."

I chuckled. "Well, I'm glad you saw through that bullshit story and knew I'd never do that to you when—"

"Wait, wait, wait. You think *that's* what tipped me off?" he asked incredulously. "You think that I didn't believe her because I thought you had some sense of honor? Some finely developed moral code?"

"Hey, now. I'm telling you, I didn't come onto her. In fact—"

"I knew she was making it up, dumbass, but it sure as hell wasn't because I wouldn't put it past you. It was completely the opposite actually. In all the wretched luck I've had with women ever since we started flying together, I never met one yet that you couldn't steal from me. Somehow, I didn't think Kell was that one either. I figured she was only telling me that because she was trying to get rid of you, and the only reason I could think of for her to do that is if she really did know what was going on." He extended his hand for the bottle of scotch, which I passed to him.

"Okay," I said, feeling my face going red. "A couple of things. First off, I've never stolen any of your—not intentionally, I mean except… Well, I mean… Nobody that you were really serious about—I mean… those times were all different is what I'm saying. You know, because… Um… Well, yeah, I mean."

He raised a quizzical eyebrow as if to say oh really and drank another swig of scotch.

"Know what? I think I'll just let that one go," I said, nodding.

"Good idea."

He passed me back the bottle of scotch.

"You coulda told me, at least," I said.

"I know, but seeing you sweat was just too much damn fun."

"Fuck you."

He chuckled. "Surely you concede you deserve it."

"Look, you let me handle my karmic accounts and you just worry about yours. How about that?"

"Fine. And now, to work on your karmic accounts, you're gonna finally get this stupid container open."

"All right, all right," I said as I stood, stamping out my cigarette butt. I'd planned to use the cold snips to cut off the diamondite locks, throw the slag blanket over the explosive anti-tamper bolt, and then cut the door around it free with the plasma cutter. "I'll have this thing open in a coupla minutes."

"Get on it then," the boss said from the floor. "I'm gonna sit here, drink scotch, hold my aching head, and watch you actually do something useful for a change."

"Yeah, yeah, yeah," I muttered, pulling on the safety gloves.

I clamped cold snips around the top lock, applied pressure, and pressed the cryo button on the grips. Jets of liquid nitrogen spat from the pliers' jaws, frosting the slate-gray diamondite to a dull white. A few seconds of chilling and pressure, and the diamondite shattered.

"One down," I said.

"You know what, though?" he asked as I maneuvered the hose linking the snips to the cryo tank in preparation to cut the second lock. "I'm really kind of glad she's gone. I mean, don't get me wrong, she was fun, but ultimately, in the end, she tried to kill me."

"Uh-huh," I said as I fiddled with the setting on the cryo tank.

"Yeah, man. I couldn't give a fuck where she went, honestly." He took another shot of scotch.

I gave him a skeptical look. I'd heard enough of these conversations in my life to recognize after-the-fact, post-breakup, several-shots-in bullshit rationalizations. The second lock gave way.

"Two down."

"In fact, I don't think I'm ever gonna think about her again," he said. "You know? Even if she sent me a message or some bullshit, I wouldn't even read it. I'd just straight up delete it."

I considered the Dear John letter in my pocket.

"So, if she like sent you a note or a letter or—"

"Fuck that noise, man," he said with a wave of his hand. "We're done and she tried to shoot me!

You think I want to read anything she has to say? No way."

I nodded but didn't answer, focusing instead on the third lock, which shattered just as easily as the other two had. After that, I adjusted the cold snips, chilled the explosive bolt as best I could, and threw the slag blanket over it, hoping it was thick enough to stop the shrapnel from killing me if I fucked up the next part of the plan.

I didn't, and five minutes' more work saw the explosive anti-tamper bolt fall free of the door. I wrapped it in the slag blanket and gingerly carried it outside where I tossed it into a nearby ditch.

When I got back, the boss staggered to his feet and handed me the bottle of scotch.

"That stuff is shitty," he said. "But it works."

"Yep." I took a pull. "Now for the moment of truth."

I disengaged the travel locks, pried the handle open, and swung the door out, only to be rewarded with a slightly smaller internal door, the type I recognized from other shipments as the kind of deep-space survivable container used for shipping valuable live animals, exotic foods, or other premium cargo.

"Maybe Liz really is shipping a tiger?" I cracked, remembering my joke to Kell a few nights ago.

"We'd better hope not," the boss answered. "In our shape, we're cat food for sure."

I opened the inner door, and the boss and I stepped inside.

The container was unlit, but light streaming in from our ship's open cargo ramp revealed that the long, heavily insulated cargo container was empty, save for a few boxy shapes at the far end, barely visible in the semi-darkness due to the faint glow of status lights.

The boss and I walked ten meters in. Wiring connected the strange system on the outside of the crate with several of the boxy shapes inside. Even standing right next to the metal and plastic system—and they had to be a system because wires and hoses connected the boxes—didn't give me much of a clue as to what I was looking at.

"Huh, check that out," the boss said, and pointed to a tall vertical computer cabinet lit by blinking green status lights. The name on the side said *Prism Medical Systems, an Ito-Tenson Company.*

I'd thought that getting the shipping container open would make things suddenly make sense, but instead, I was more confused than ever. Whatever medical equipment this stuff was had to be expensive, but it couldn't be worth that much money, and certainly wouldn't be worth putting a sizeable bounty on. I looked around in the semi-darkness and noticed a two-meter-long horizontal cabinet that had letters stenciled on top. I bent low to read them: *PATIENT ACCESS*.

A pair of latches held the top of the cabinet in place. I opened them both and slid the cover back—and about jumped out of my skin.

"Holy shit, boss," I whispered, pointing to what I'd found.

He took a look and turned pale. "We are so fucked."

There, under glass and connected to various IVs and status monitors, lay a sleeping Michael Ver.

CHAPTER SIXTEEN

I awoke the next morning feeling like I hadn't slept at all. Despite the boss changing the cargo hatch access code and leaving the ship's navigation computer and primary systems powered up in case we had to make a break for it, I'd still woken up at least once an hour, paranoid that Kell and company were coming for us in the middle of the night. The knowledge that we had a knocked-out, drugged-up pop star on life support in the hold didn't help either.

The boss was already awake, sitting in the cockpit, taking advantage of our net connection to check out news on Michael Ver. I smoked a cigarette and ate an energy bar on our ratty blue couch while he scanned the headlines.

"'*Michael Ver Missing: LoVers Distraught,*'" he read. "The article says he'd had problems with his label, and they think he may be on some sort of strike or whatever until he gets what he wants. Another one speculates that he's in rehab. A couple of other sites seem to think he met a girl and got married or joined some religious group. So far, nobody seems to think he's been kidnapped. I dunno if that's good or bad."

"Well, since there's a bounty for the return of the box, obviously somebody knows what's really going on," I said. "But that still doesn't explain the other contract to destroy it. I mean, the dude is worth millions—maybe more. What sense would it be to kill him when a ransom would make you a fortune?"

"I dunno, Snake. Maybe he pissed somebody off bad enough to where they just want him gone. The dude is a prick, you know."

"Well, yeah, but just because somebody's a prick doesn't mean a contract gets put out on 'em. I mean—"

"Yeah, you're still walking around, aren't you?"

I chuckled. "Exactly."

"Uh-oh, Snake. Here's something else. This is from PStarz—one of those stupid celebrity sites. Listen to this: '*PStarz has confirmed Ver had trouble with a pair of locals on Yaeger, where he was punched in a dispute in a club during the filming for his upcoming single 'Baby, Baby.' Further, sources tell PStarz that one of them was seen later in Ver's hotel, armed with a gun and that there may have been shots fired. John 'Liz' Nellis, Michael Ver's head of security, confirmed police are still looking for the mysterious men, but refused to answer any other questions about Ver's whereabouts. Is it possible Michael Ver is in hiding, fearing for his life?'"*

"That fucking bastard," I said. "Liz knows exactly what happened, but he's letting them pin that shit on us. Plus, Liz should be dead, Jesus. Motherfucker's got more lives than a litter of kittens."

"How much you wanna bet that was the plan the whole time?" the boss mused. "Liz knew people would recognize us from the club and we'd be natural suspects, and used Kell to get close to us. Then, I bet the idea was to get us to the hotel and have us arrested, while Ver disappears along with our ship."

"What good does that do him? If we're arrested, how could we have anything to do with Ver being gone?"

"Simple," he said. "The stupid Holloway cops would never believe us, and they'd just keep sweating us to tell them where 'the rest of the gang' was or something."

"Jesus, that's a complicated-ass plan. Sounds like something you'd come up with, honestly. Are you sure you didn't have anything to do with this?" I asked with a grin.

"A complicated plan doesn't mean it's a bad plan, Snake. Just because you don't get it doesn't mean the rest of us don't."

I snorted. "No, what makes it a bad plan is the fact that we're sitting here with Ver on life support instead of Liz."

"And that still doesn't explain why they wanted him to disappear. And for how long?" the boss said, scrolling through more news.

"Or who wants Ver dead," I reminded him.

"You know, this kind of stuff never used to happen to me before I hired you," he said.

"Oh no, don't you go blaming this shit on me. I've never been on the wrong end of so many people trying to kill me as I have since I got hired on—and I did a three-year hard labor 'correctional tour' aboard the Braxton, remember?"

"Exactly. This is your bad karma coming back to get you, and I'm just guilty by association. Anyway, it doesn't matter. What does matter is now that we know we've got Ver, we've got to figure out the best way to turn his stupid ass into cash."

"Now you're talking. I guess killing him is right out?"

"Jesus, Snake."

"I know, I know—I just wanted to make sure I understood the ground rules."

"Well, the way I see it, we—"

The comm station beeped. The boss glanced at the computer, hit a key, and Carla's voice came through the cockpit speakers, slightly garbled by the encryption process.

"You two still alive down there?"

I smiled. If she was close enough to use the comm channel, she was only minutes away. And that meant good things, not the least of which was me and her without clothes on.

"Yeah," the boss said back. "A bit worse for the wear, but we're still kicking."

"All right, well I got news for you—your cargo has picked up some additional interest, and it's heading here, quick-like. Nav lanes are clear right now, but they won't be for long. Whatever shit you two stepped in, it smells to high heaven, apparently."

"Yeah, we know. Look, we'll explain it all when you get down here."

"Yeah, you will," Carla said. "I'll be on the ground in about ten minutes, and I brought a friend with me, so don't panic when an FRL CH-14 follows me in."

"Roger."

"Carla out." The channel closed.

"A friend, huh?" I asked, flicking my cigarette butt through the midships hatch into the cargo bay. "Maybe Carla's bringing somebody for you to rebound with, eh, bossman? Maybe even somebody that won't try to kill us both when you two break up. That'd be a nice change."

He sighed. "Fuck you, Snake."

We argued for a few more minutes until the whine of anti-grav units and the earth-shaking roar of retro rockets alerted us to inbound craft. The boss took a quick look out the cockpit.

"It's them."

"Good. By the way, does the deal I made with you and Kell about me babysitting the cargo last night and going out with Carla tonight still hold?"

His eyes narrowed, but he didn't answer.

"I'm gonna call that a 'yes,' boss."

"Get fucked."

"Yeah, that's what I'm trying to do, see, which is why I—"

"Shut up, Snake."

I chuckled and we made our way out of the midships to the cargo bay. He dropped the cargo ramp, and we trudged across the vacant spaceport toward Carla's menacing Razor and the boxy, battle-scarred freighter that was Carla's friend's CH-14.

Carla's Razor powered down first, and she climbed down from the cockpit, her flight suit as curve-hugging as ever. I smiled.

When she reached the ground, she faced the boss and me with a quizzical look, hands on her hips.

"You know," she said with a nod at me, "you are awfully needy for a guy."

"Huh? What's that supposed to mean."

"It means you're high maintenance. I've had girlfriends who required less attention than you do."

"Wait," the boss said to Carla. "You had a girlfriend? You mean like you and a girl—"

"Yeah. You'd have liked to have seen that, wouldn't you?"

He turned red, and Carla chuckled. I sighed.

"Smooth, boss. Super smooth."

"What happened to you, by the way?" Carla asked, leaning close to him. "Somebody break your nose?"

"Maybe," he said. "It's a long story."

"Oh, I'm sure. How do you two get into so much trouble anyway? What do you guys do when I'm not around?"

"The usual," the boss deadpanned.

"Oh yeah? What is that, exactly?"

"You know, smoking cigarettes and watching Captain Kangaroo," I said with a shrug.

Carla snorted. "Well, this is the second time I've had to get you out of trouble and—"

"The first time, need I remind you, the trouble you got us out of was the same trouble you got us into," the boss said pointedly.

"Oh no, don't start that again," Carla said with a shake of her head. "You got yourself into that one. I just offered you the job."

"Whatever. We didn't ask for your help this time, remember? You just volunteered."

"I guess that's right. It's just that your boy Snake here is like a sad puppy dog. I can't be gone long without worrying about him," she said.

I rolled my eyes and gave her the finger. She winked at me and mouthed later.

"God, I hate it when you two flirt," the boss said.

"It's why we do it, honestly," Carla said. "We don't even really like each other."

"You know, given my luck, I'd almost buy that."

I chuckled as I pointed to the massive CH-14, whose primary generators had powered down and had begun discharging crew out her side hatch. "What's with the freighter anyway? I didn't think cargo escort was your kind of thing."

"It's not," Carla answered. "But what was it he said? 'It's a long story'? Same here. At least my nose isn't broken."

A familiar figure made her way out of the hatch and toward us: Carla's roommate and ex—at least I thought she was an ex—girlfriend.

"Is that Jade?" I asked.

Carla looked over her shoulder. "Yeah. She's doing a tour with her latest art installment. This one's called *Manti's Girl*."

"And you just decided to escort her ship?" the boss asked incredulously.

"I think the fact that you're not drunk in a gutter on Greenly and I'm standing here trying to help you out of yet another fucking mess more than demonstrates I have a charitable side," Carla said in an icy tone far more serious than her earlier banter.

I frowned. The boss was right to be skeptical. Something didn't make sense, and whatever it was,

Carla obviously didn't want to talk about it. Part of me wondered whether Carla and Jade were back together, which must have shown on my face, because Carla rolled her eyes at me.

"No, Snake, you don't have anything to worry about. You're still safe."

Damn, did she know me well.

Jade was now close enough to realize who Carla was talking to, and the look on her face told me she was no more thrilled to see me than the last time we'd talked. She scowled as she marched closer, hands folded across her chest—which was probably a good thing, because her gauzy blue top was distractingly sheer, and I couldn't see any bra straps. I had the good sense to keep my eyes off her with Carla so close, but the boss had no such compunction, although he did better than he normally did, to be fair.

"These two?" Jade sighed. "You set us down on this rock for Snake and… him?" She pointed at the boss. "What do they want?"

"Hey now, Carla contacted us, not the other way around," the boss said.

"I knew I should have cut off your access to my account, Carla," Jade fumed.

Carla rolled her eyes. "Jade, could we not have this conversation, again, right here, right now?"

There was uncomfortable silence for a few seconds before the boss broke it up.

"So, uh, Jade, Carla said you were traveling with your art exhibit?"

Jade snorted. "Is that what she said? Because that's not exactly true, is it, Carla? Actually, the—"

"*Jade*," Carla warned.

"Damn it, Carla, I'll say what I goddamn well please. I think I've earned that right. Carla's in some trouble, and we're on the move."

Carla's posture stiffened for a second, but she gave a nonchalant shrug. "Nothing I can't handle."

Oh yeah, there was definitely something going on, all right. My eyes met the boss's, and I saw the wheels in his head turning.

"Trouble, eh? Anything we can help with?" he asked Jade.

Inside, I smiled. On the rebound already. Good on you.

Jade turned to Carla. "Well?"

"I said I could handle it."

Jade sighed. "Apparently not, but thanks for asking. Better than Snake here, who's Carla's 'boyfriend' and didn't even bother."

That fucking bitch.

"Look, I didn't ask because if Carla said she's got it, then that's fucking good enough for me.

Have a little faith." It came out a little harsher than I meant it to, but I'll be damned if I was going to let Jade's frustration mess up what me and Carla had going on.

Jade shot me a lethal look but addressed Carla instead. "Well, whenever you get done with whatever it is you've got here, I'll be on the *Golden Fang*." She stomped off back toward the CH-14.

The boss shook his head at me, sighed, looked at us, back at Jade, and then back at us before he took off after Jade. "Fill her in for me, would you, Snake?" he said over his shoulder.

"Sure."

"Hurry back. I don't have much time," Carla called as she watched the boss fall in beside Jade.

"What's that mean?" I asked.

"You two have about ten hours before the rest of the hunters out there looking for you realize the tip I fed some of my sources saying I'd seen you on the Balto-Riga route was wrong. And I've got about four hours before I've got to get the *Golden Fang* back in the air."

"Four hours, huh? That's it? So, you *are* in trouble."

"No. Not trouble, per se. It's just that in my line of work, you have to be ready to move because sometimes you make enemies. Jade knows that, but every time it happens, she flips the fuck out."

"So why does she keep coming with you? I mean, aside from—"

"This time was a little different," Carla admitted. "It was probably best for Jade's safety if she left Greenly as well."

I studied Carla's face, trying to read how big a deal whatever it was she was involved in really was, but her eyes betrayed nothing. She gave me a half smirk and pulled a cigarette from her flight suit. I offered her a light, which she took. I waited for her to explain more about the situation, but she smoked in silence.

"So—seriously—do you need some help?" I asked, realizing she wasn't going to volunteer anything on her own.

"Snake, I have to admit I'm flattered by the fact that I can help you discover your deeply hidden gentlemanly side. It's sweet, but I promise, I don't need your help. Remember when I said my past was mine?"

"Yeah."

"It still is."

I shrugged. "That's fair enough, but how do you know I'm offering you help 'cause I'm feeling gentlemanly? I could have ulterior motives." I grinned.

"Oh, I'd say that's a given," she replied with a smirk.

"You know me so well. Tell you what, I got the very last sip or two of a bottle of shitty scotch left and something to show you in the cargo bay that's gonna blow your fucking mind." I nodded back toward our Black Sun 490.

"I remember the last time you said you had something in the bay to show me, on Rucker Watson's," she said, a gleam in her eye.

I grinned. "Of course you do, because I believe the last time I said that, I showed you what we in the biz call 'a good time.'"

She laughed as we headed to the ship. "And this time?"

"Same plan, eventually. But first, you probably ought to know we have a guest."

"For real?"

"You could say he's our third crew member, although he was our fourth for a while, we just didn't know it."

"Say what?"

"Oh, it's fucking great," I said. "You ever hear of a dude named Michael Ver?"

"The singer?"

"Yeah, that's the guy."

CHAPTER SEVENTEEN

"You have got to be fucking kidding me," Carla said when I showed her Ver asleep in his glass coffin.

"Unfortunately, no."

"And exactly how did this happen again?"

I shrugged. "I already told you. Ver stole the coat. We got the coat back, my boy picked up a girlfriend, and then it all sorta went to hell."

Carla shook her head. "It's a wonder you two aren't dead already." She sighed. "Although actually knowing what's in here makes some sense."

"Huh? How?"

"The bounty," Carla said. "I did a little digging on the bounty with some contacts of mine when Jade and I stopped on Riga II. The 'return cargo undamaged' bounty is offered by Maple Mutual and Trust. It's an insurance company. Must be the one that insures Ver."

"Okay, so it makes sense they want him back alive, I guess," I said. "But why not just tell everybody what's going on in the first place? I mean, if they want him back, why not say he's missing and offer a reward? Why the bounty?"

"I dunno. And it also doesn't explain who wants him dead."

"You'd understand if you'd've met him," I said. "Trust me on that. He's a little shit."

"No doubt. All the pretty ones are."

I frowned. "So, what's that say about me?"

Carla laughed. "You figure it out, genius."

"Hey, I'll have you know that lots of girls find me pretty good looking," I protested.

"And you can find them all in the Cedar Pines head injury ward."

"Har har."

"Aww," she said sarcastically. "Did I hurt your feelings? I'm sure I can make it up to you."

"It's all good," I said, pulling her close and putting my arms around her waist.

God, did I have great ideas about what was going to happen next.

Unfortunately, the universe had other ideas, because two hard knocks on the cargo bay hatch fucked up my plans for fucking.

I sighed. "You're fine," I called.

The hydraulic pump whined and the rear cargo hatch opened, revealing the boss, arms crossed. At least he'd knocked this time. The last time he'd dropped the ramp unexpectedly when Carla and I were alone during a brief layover on Tayir, he'd seen a bit more than he'd wanted to.

"You got great timing. Anybody ever tell you that?" I said.

"Not my fucking problem if you're too slow, Snake."

"And that—that right there—is why you can't get a girl."

"Snake," he warned.

I shrugged. "Just trying to help, that's all. Speaking of help, how'd it go with Jade?"

"Not your concern. What is concerning is what Jade told me."

"And that was what, exactly?" Carla asked.

"She said you were gonna be outta here in like three or four hours."

"She's right. Which is why Snake here was just filling me in on the giant fucking mess you two got yourselves into."

"Uh-huh. I bet you were going to do some 'filling in' for sure," he said as he strode up the ramp. "But the thing is, I can't trust Snake to remember anything you've said afterward, so I figured I'd better come back and figure out exactly what the hell you know about all this."

He was probably right, honestly, but that didn't make me any less pissed off.

"The bounty for Ver's safe return is offered by an insurance company," I told him. "So that's probably who Liz and Kell wanted to sell him off to. I think they were gonna kidnap him and then ransom him, but we fucked their plans up."

"See, now that's useful information," he said.

"Okay, so now that you've got it, how 'bout you turn the fuck around and get lost?" I said.

He didn't answer, instead walking past us into the midships and settling down in the cockpit.

"Soooo?" Carla asked.

"So which company was it? I'll send 'em a message. We tell 'em we got their man, explain the situation to them, collect the bounty, and we're in the money."

"Maple Mutual and Trust," Carla said. "But you got a lot of people between you and them. I don't think it's gonna be quite that simple."

The boss typed on his keyboard and then muttered a string of curses.

"What?" I asked.

"Oh, 'it's not gonna be that simple' is the motherfucking understatement of the year," he said through clenched teeth.

"What?"

"Have a look."

Carla and I made our way to the midships and crowded behind the pilot's seat so we could see the screen over the boss's shoulder.

On it was the "about us" page of the Maple Mutual and Trust Corporation. The executive VP of special projects was a familiar gorgeous redhead with a winning smile.

Shit.

"Whoa. She's cute," Carla said. "What's her name?"

I put my head in my hands. "Her name is Kell."

"Kell?" Carla asked. "Isn't that the name of the—"

"Yeah, that's her," the boss said. "And now everything makes even less sense. Hell, we don't—" A look of sudden inspiration crossed his face, and his eyes went wide.

"Oh, no," I said, shaking my head. "I know that look. That's the 'I've got what I think is a great idea that's actually a colossal fuckup that's probably gonna get us killed' look. Whatever it is, you can forget about it, because—"

"No, listen. I've got it. I've got our way out."

"Well, let's hear it then, flyboy," Carla said.

"It's simple," the boss said. "We sell Ver back to Kell, then boom, she's got what she wants, the insurance company pulls the bounty, and we're good to go."

"I can see about a million problems with that plan," I said. "First, how are you going to get back in touch with Kell? Second, what makes you think we can trust her to deliver anything to us? She's more likely to wait us out until her crew makes it here, then swing by the ship, fuck us up, and *take* Ver back, not pay us for him. And last, but definitely not least, what about the other assholes out there with the kill bounty? 'Cause I bet even when Ver goes back, Kell and company don't bother to tell whoever it is wants Ver dead that they've got him, which means we're still gonna have bounty hunters waiting at every jump point ready to punch us in the throat."

"Because of that container," he answered with a grin. "We're gonna give both sides what they want."

"And how the fuck is that gonna work?"

"Schrödinger's cat," Carla answered, with the look of dawning comprehension in her eyes.

"Exactly," the boss said. "That's exactly it."

"Whatever," I said.

Carla gave me an impish smile. "You don't get it, do you?"

I didn't, but of course I'm not stupid enough to admit it.

"Oh, I get it," I said. "It's just not going to work." Even without understanding the plan, I pretty much figured it not working was a given.

"Okay then, Snake, what's your idea?" the boss asked.

I shrugged. "Planning's not my department. I never claimed to know when shit was gonna work—I just know when it won't."

"Helpful as ever, man," the boss said. "But since you don't have any better ideas, we're gonna do it my way this time."

"Uh, we pretty much always do it your way, I'd just like to point out."

"That's 'cause the last time we did it your way, her boyfriend and his crew almost killed you, and I had to come in guns blazing to get you out of that fucking restaurant and then we all got arrested, remember?" the boss asked.

Carla gave me an *oh really?* look that told me she had missile lock and I had about point-three seconds before she pulled the trigger.

I held up a hand and counted my points off on my fingers. "First, that was a long time ago—before I met Carla, obviously." I glanced at her to make sure she understood the timeline. "Secondly, I was fine. It was a tense situation, but I had it under control until you started shooting. And third, how the fuck was I supposed to know he was gonna show up?"

"I dunno. Maybe because he owned the place, like I fucking told you he did?"

"Well, I mean, yeah, I guess, but it was supposed to be his night off."

Carla shook her head. "I've said it before, and I'll say it again—I don't know how you two dumb fucks are still alive."

"We're very resilient," the boss said. "You know, like… like…."

"Like cockroaches?" Carla said with a chuckle.

"Sure, like cockroaches. Whatever. Anyway, you've only got a few hours left on the ground and we're gonna need your help, I think."

"How's that?"

"Because once we wake him up and I—"

"Whoa, there," I interrupted. "Slow the fuck down. We're waking him up? Why the hell would we do that?"

Carla and the boss stared at me like I was the dumbest man alive.

"Of course we are, Snake," he said. "How the fuck else would it work?"

I just shrugged, since I didn't really understand what the plan was anyway because I had no clue who this Schrödinger was—or what the hell his fucking cat had to do with anything.

"So, like I was saying," the boss continued, "once we wake him up, I'm gonna need you to scout out my meetup spot with Kell and watch my back. She'll be expecting Snake, but I'll tell her I'm coming alone, and she'll never suspect you're with me."

"For good reason," Carla said dryly.

He scowled.

"And what about me?" I asked.

"You stay here and watch Ver until Kell and I make a deal. Then, we come back here, get his stupid ass, and hand him over to Kell for cash, obviously."

I still didn't get why we didn't hand the container over or how this idea was going to get us out from under the other bounty, but at least this portion made sense. I did have one troubling thought, though.

"Uh, does anybody know how to wake him up?"

CHAPTER EIGHTEEN

Fortunately, you can look almost anything up on the net, so we were able to find a copy of a manual for a model pretty close to the one we had in the container. In fact, we found a manual for the exact model too, but that manual cost fifteen credits, and we weren't gonna buy a fucking electronic manual for fifteen credits for a single use, somebody's life on the line or not—that's highway fucking robbery.

"All right," I said, checking the switch settings one last time. "I think we're good to go here."

I looked over my shoulder in the dark container at the boss, who consulted his laptop and typed in some instructions on a small touchscreen on Ver's chamber. "The settings look right here, too, I think. So, looks like once I initiate the process, it'll hit him with the stims in a minute or two, then with a minor steroid shot to overcome any lost muscle mass, and he'll start coming around."

"He's gonna freak out, you know," Carla said from the container door. "You'd better watch it when he wakes up."

"Eh," the boss said with a shrug. "I took him down when he was ready for a fight. I'm not too worried about him waking up after a coma. Here goes." He flipped a switch and touched something on the screen.

The computer cabinet closest to me gave a soft chime, and a few lights went from blue to green. The boss slid the cover back from Ver, put his ear to the glass case around the sleeping pop star, and nodded.

"The air circulation is changing," he said. "We did it right. Won't be long now."

Indeed, it wasn't.

Ver's eyes snapped open, a look of sheer terror on his face. He yanked the tube out of his nose and mouth, ripping out IV lines and spraying the inside of the glass with blood as he did so. He tried to sit up, hit his head on the case, and yelped in pain.

"Chill out! Just calm down!" the boss yelled.

A look of recognition crossed Ver's face, followed by rage. "You!" he shouted, voice muffled by the glass. "What the fuck are you doing? It was a coat, man!"

"Calm down," the boss ordered. "This isn't about the fuckin' coat. Now just—"

"N-n-not about the coat?" Ver sputtered. He looked confused for a moment, then horrified. "Oh god, I promise I wasn't gonna testify. Really! I just told 'em I would so they'd let me go!"

"What the fuck are you talking about?" I asked. "Just do like he said and calm down. We don't care about any testimony or whatever."

"Do you work for Mikey and Melvin?" Ver asked. "I'll pay—I told 'em I would, and I will, okay? I promise I will, as soon as I get the advance for the next single. I promise!"

"Jesus! Stop your panicking, okay?" the boss said. "Seriously. Just shut up for half a second and we'll get you out. We aren't going to hurt you."

I reflected on the truth of that statement, considering we were planning on handing him right back over to the people who'd kidnapped him to start with, but, hey, you're either the dog or you're the dog food, right?

When Ver calmed down, the boss and I opened the glass and helped him out into the container. Carla gave him an appreciative once-over as he stood there in his underwear, which drew an eye roll from me and a chuckle from the boss. We tossed him some ill-fitting sweatpants and a red, worn-out long-sleeved T-shirt. Ver tugged on the pants but didn't put on the shirt. Instead, he tied it around his waist and checked out his reflection in the glass. I groaned.

"All right, so here's how this is gonna work, okay?" the boss said after we marched Ver into the cargo bay. "All you gotta do is exactly what we say, and then you can get back to fucking pretty girls and singing *'baby baby baby'* or whatever, got it? Just listen and follow instructions."

"Bullshit," Ver said, hands on his hips. Apparently, putting on clothes had given him back his asshole confidence. "You two aren't gonna just kidnap me, fly me to god knows where, and then give me a set of orders without explaining stuff first. You two psychos might be trying to get me killed. Start talking."

"You must be new to this, shit-for-brains," Carla said, arms crossed. "When you're one unarmed wannabe tough guy two minutes removed from hibernation surrounded by three armed motherfuckers, you don't get to make demands."

Ver seemed to notice Carla for the first time. He gave her a dismissive snort. "Yo, whose chick is this?"

My mouth dropped open, and the boss winced.

"What the fuck did you just say?" Carla asked, taking a menacing step toward Ver. Her right hand disappeared inside her coat. "The fuck was it you just called me? Somebody's chick?"

Ver opened his mouth but never got a word out, because it's hard to talk when somebody's got the barrel of a 10mm auto shoved between your teeth.

"Mmmmmf! Mmm!" Ver said, eyes wide in panic.

"Now, listen to me, you limp-dicked little punk," Carla said. "I am nobody's 'chick.' I am here on my own. I originally came to help out these two, but now I'm thinking that the eighty-four-grand bounty for your corpse is looking mighty attractive—and if you think this pistol is uncomfortable now, just wait till I fit it somewhere else, got it?"

She withdrew the pistol from his mouth and cuffed him upside the head with it—not hard enough to knock him out, but enough to send him to his knees in pain.

"Well," the boss said. "Looks like we've all learned a valuable lesson. So where were we? Oh yeah, I remember—you were gonna keep your fucking mouth shut while we explained what you were gonna do."

Ver nodded as he staggered to his feet, still reeling from his encounter with Carla.

"So, Ca—" The boss's mouth snapped shut when he realized he'd almost said Carla's name in front of Ver. "So, our female associate here and I are going to meet somebody who—for some reason—is willing to pay money to get your stupid ass back."

"And in the meantime, you'll be staying here with me," I said. "Where you'll be on your best goddamned behavior, else I'll hand you over to her when she gets back." I pointed to Carla and grinned.

"And that about sums it up. Any questions?" the boss asked.

Ver nodded.

"Seriously? You've got a question?" Carla asked.

"Uh, yeah, actually," Ver said in a tone that sounded nigh close to respectful. "Who's paying to get me back? If they're gonna k-kill me, I can pay you guys whatever. Just don't give me over to Mikey's folks, or the Sparrows, or the—"

"Jesus," I said. "And I thought we had enemies."

"I guess that explains the bounty for your death," the boss said. "Who all have you pissed off?"

"Ahhh… Well, the Sparrows are after me because when we were filming a video on Haska-Yan, they busted one of their guys—my Z dealer— with a load of product. And they got me with him, so I said I'd testify, but I really wasn't, I promise— I'm no snitch, know what I mean?"

"Uh-huh," I said. "Because when I think of people who aren't snitches, I definitely think of people who volunteer to testify."

"I didn't, though! I bugged out before the trial date, and I haven't been back to Haska-Yan since then."

"Yeah, but apparently the Sparrows haven't forgotten, because there's definitely a bounty out for you," the boss said. "And, oh by the way, since Haska-Yan's not in the UNF, you don't have to worry about the UNF boys coming for you, but last I heard, the government of Haska-Yan is pretty harsh, so they probably just tried you in absentia and declared you guilty—with a death sentence."

"Oh," Ver said, his face falling. "Shit." He thought for a moment. "And, uh… Also, I owe this guy Mikey and his boy Mel a bunch of money too."

"What kind of business are they in?" Carla asked.

"The, uh, 'girl business,' I guess you could say?" Ver winced.

"And how much do you owe 'em?" Carla asked as she lit a cigarette.

"Call it two or three hundred large? We had a coupla big release parties they set us up with girls for and, uh, I never really paid 'em, I guess."

"You are well and truly fucked, you know that?" Carla said with a laugh.

Ver nodded. "But that's why I hired Liz and his crew. Of course, a lot of fucking good it did me," he said, scowling at me and the boss.

"Ain't that the truth," I said. "And here's a tip for you—you might wanna get rid of Liz too, if you see him again."

"Wait. What's that mean?" Ver asked.

"You figure it out, dipshit," the boss said. "Doesn't matter anyway. Bottom line is, we're handing you over to your insurance company, and they appear to want you back in one piece, so whatever beef you got with them, you two can settle it shortly."

"I don't understand. Why would I have a beef with my own—"

The hydraulic pump and lowering cargo bay ramp drowned out the rest of Ver's question. The boss threw on his shoulder holster and walked down the ramp, Carla following.

"So how are you gonna find Kell?" I asked.

The boss turned around at the base of the ramp. "Don't worry about that, Snake. You just keep a watch on our Teen Beat heartthrob here and make sure he doesn't go anywhere."

I glanced over at Ver, who sat on the floor of the cargo bay, head in his hands.

"Not too worried about that," I said.

"It's not him you need to worry about," Carla pointed out. "It's whoever else might come looking for him."

"You two just hurry back so we can get this thing done with," I said. *And because I still want some time with Carla alone,* I didn't add.

They headed across the spaceport, and I closed the cargo bay.

CHAPTER NINETEEN

I was sitting on the couch in the midships next to the open hatch leading to the cargo bay — smoking a cigarette and reassembling the spare water pump I'd just gotten done repairing — when I heard a clatter in the cargo bay and Ver's cry of surprise.

I poked my head into the bay.

"What the fuck are you doing?" I asked. "I told you not to mess with anything." I swore under my breath. I'd already cut off the circuit breaker leading to the rear hydraulic pump, so even if he were able to figure out how to drop the rear door, he couldn't, and I'd done a brief scan of the bay before I went amidships to verify there was nothing hanging around that he could use to hurt me. What was he up to?

Ver didn't answer.

"Yo, did you not hear me?"

Again, there was no response.

"All right, motherfucker," I said. "Have it your way. But there's no place to hide, and the bay ain't that fucking big, but keep it up, because I'm about to tie you up. And if I catch you over at the maintenance access hatch, I'm gonna beat you to within an inch of your life, too."

I walked into the bay, knife at the ready, just in case he'd suddenly grown a set of balls and had decided he was going to jump out at me wielding a gallon bucket of turboshaft oil or a spare filter box or something. A quick glance told me the maintenance hatch was undisturbed, which I was glad about, because that was about the only place he could really cause a problem by messing with, even if I didn't think he'd have a clue how to get it open.

"Come on out, Ver," I said, creeping down the side of his shipping container. "I don't know what you think you're up to, but you'd better start talking, because all we need is you alive—not necessarily in good shape."

As I made my way around the container, I glanced behind me, making sure he wasn't attempting to sneak around and get into the midships, trying to escape through the forward hatch the way I'd done on San Pierre.

Still no sign of Ver.

"Look, you stupid motherfucker," I called out. "I've been on this ship for years now, and there's no way you're gonna hide from me in the cargo bay—all you're gonna do is piss me off, and when I find you, you're gonna regret it."

The container doors hung open more widely than I'd last seen, and I saw the T-shirt we'd given Ver just inside. I stepped partway into the dark container, squinting at the medical system lights at the end.

"I've got my knife out," I told the darkness. "So, if you think you're gonna hide out back there and jump out at me, you might wanna think *reeeal* hard about it before you do."

As my eyes adjusted, I could barely make out an unfamiliar shape sticking out around the side of a far computer cabinet. *Gotcha, motherfucker.* I took another step inside.

A sharp shove in my back sent me stumbling forward into the darkness, and my stomach knotted as the container door slammed shut with a metallic clang.

I scrambled toward the door, but the clink-clunk sound of the turning latch told me I was locked inside.

Fuck.

———————————

The soundproofed walls gave me no clue as to what was going on outside the container, and I had no idea how much time had passed. So when the door suddenly opened to reveal the boss and Carla silhouetted by the open cargo bay, I nearly had a heart attack.

I blinked in the cargo bay lights. "Soooo, how's everything with Kell?"

"Motherfucker, I am going to kill you," the boss said.

"Whoa, whoa, whoa," I said, holding up my hand to shield my eyes so I could see the boss's face. "Let's not lose our minds here. It's a setback, but it's no big deal."

"Not a 'big deal?' Not a 'big deal?'" he shouted. "I just worked out an exchange for eighty grand and come back to find him gone and you locked up and it's not a big deal? Are you out of your goddamn mind? It's not a 'big deal,' it's the biggest of all possible deals, you stupid fuck!"

"We'll get him back, boss. He can't have gone far, and—"

"How long have you been in there?" Carla asked.

I shrugged. "I dunno. Don't have a watch."

"How 'bout an estimate, Snake?" the boss sneered. "A little bit of time, a long time?"

"Ahhh…"

"How the ever-loving fuck did this happen?" the boss said, staring at the container. "How did he overpower you and get you in here—I mean, really? How does this—I just—like, I don't even know how—" He kicked the steel wall, threw his hands into the air, and stomped away.

I sighed. "Well, stuff happens, you know?"

"How'd he get the drop on you when you still had your knife?" Carla asked as she pointed to my E-14 in its sheath.

"Like I said, it's just one of those—"

"Wait. Did he trick you into getting in there and then close the door behind you or something?" Carla said, a mischievous light in her eyes.

"No," I lied.

She laughed. "That is what happened, isn't it? Oh, Snake, I'm not gonna let you hear the end of this one for a—"

"That's not what happened!" I protested.

"Snake, you know how I can tell when you're lying?" she asked.

"He's talking?" the boss growled.

"Pretty much," she said.

"Hey, I can fix this," I said, desperate to move the topic of conversation to a new subject. "It'll be easy."

"Oh really?" the boss said. "And how exactly are you gonna do that, Snake? What kind of crazy bullshit Snake magic are you gonna use to figure out where Ver ran off to, especially since I have…" He checked his wrist. "…exactly one fucking hour to have him back to Kell? So, let's hear it."

I racked my brain. "So, I'll just—ah—well, see, I'll go to the meet location and…"

"And? Go on, I'm listening."

"And then… I'll…" My mind raced. "I'll, uh… steal the money from Kell… before she's ready to make the exchange." I blinked in surprise. Even though—as usual—my mouth moved faster than my brain, the plan actually made sense.

"Say what?" the boss asked.

"I think I get it," Carla said. "Snake goes to the meet early and swipes Kell's cash, then runs his ass back here, you two take off, I take off, and we're gone. Then, you run the rest of the plan like before and boom, you're clear."

"You mean, except for that Kell and company still want us dead," the boss said.

"Obviously."

"It's either that or we run *and* Kell keeps the money," I said. "Because you were right—I have no fucking clue where Ver went, or how to find him."

"You don't even know if she'll be at the meet early," the boss protested.

"Sure, I do. You were planning on being there early and staking it out, right? Just to make sure some friends of hers weren't gonna jump you, right? She'll be doing the same thing."

"Yeah, but the thing is, the whole reason I was going early was because I wanted to be cautious and on guard, which means if she's early, she's going to be the same way."

"C'mon, boss," I said. "Have a little confidence in me."

Carla laughed. "Now that is a ballsy request, given recent events."

I smiled. "Of course, it is. That's why you like me."

CHAPTER TWENTY

The alley where I waited for Kell was a dusty narrow thing filled with trash from the restaurant on one side and broken kids' toys from an apartment complex on the other. Crouched behind a dumpster, I smoked a cigarette to calm my nerves and mask the smell of garbage as I waited for the blue four-door sedan whose backseat Carla had spotted Kell getting out of during her previous meet with the boss. Across the street was a tiny city green space decorated with a statue of the colony's founder and a plaque or two commemorating something I'm sure the locals found important. From my foul-smelling hiding place, I had a good view of the actual meet location—an empty bench next to a small commemorative fountain in the park.

Behind me, just north of the alley on the street that paralleled the street I surveilled, Carla was in a rented pickup truck, waiting to run me back to the ship. Overall, I estimated my chances of actually being able to steal the money and make it back to the ship alive at about fifteen percent—in other words, well within normal risk parameters for one of our plans.

A red sports car passed the entrance to the alley and disappeared, but I heard brakes and doors opening. Footsteps on the pavement grew louder, and I had just enough time to duck down behind the dumpster before whoever had been in the sports car made it to the alley entrance.

"Whatcha think?" a low male voice asked.

"Fuck this shit, man," a gravelly female voice answered. "She's just paranoid. There's only two of 'em, she said, and he came alone the first time."

"Right there with you, Gina," the male voice answered. "I'm gonna call it up that we're clear."

"I don't get why she just doesn't do the meet and stamp the fuck who's trying to sell Ver back to us, but I've only been doing this for ten years, so what do I know?"

The male voice snorted. "Hell if I get it either, but Liz said to listen to Kell, and Kell said nobody gets hurt, so that's the deal. Whole world's gone fucking soft."

"Yeah, I know. Damn shame."

"Kell, we're good. Me and Gina are at the alley, and it's clear too." I figured the man must have been talking on a comms net or phone. "What's that?" he asked. "Yeah, there's nothing out there. You and Paco are clear to move in. We're moving back to our spot."

I heard more footsteps, doors closing, and then the sound of tires on asphalt as the car pulled away. Breathing a sigh of relief, I peeked out around the dumpster to verify one of them hadn't stayed behind in the alley.

I was alone.

Only a minute or two later, a blue late-model four-door with a rental holo tag pulled up and parked directly across from me, blocking the alley, with the driver's door opposite my position. I gave a soft chuckle—if this was Kell's car, she could hardly have made it any easier.

The driver's door opened and a short, muscular man in dark cargo pants and a tight T-shirt stepped out. I frowned. He couldn't have been more obviously hired muscle if he'd had a shirt on that said *1-800-GOONS-FOR-RENT*. Just as he was about to close the door, he leaned back down, as if listening to an instruction from the back seat.

"I got it, Kell," he snapped. "And remember, you may be paying the bills, but you ain't my boss, so watch your tone, okay?"

He closed the door harder than was necessary and stomped off across the street toward the park.

I crouched low and moved as quickly and quietly as I could to the car's rear passenger door. So close to the car's mirror-tinted windows, I could just make out the back of Kell's head as she stared at the park bench. I drew my knife and took a deep breath.

"Here goes nothing," I muttered, and yanked open the car door.

Kell's eyes widened in shock as I clamped a hand across her mouth and pushed her across the seat far enough for me to get in before I closed the door. I pressed the lock button with my knife hand and listened for the car doors' click before I removed my hand from Kell's mouth.

"Well, hello there, Kell. You look surprised to see me."

Her lips pressed into a thin line, and anger flashed across her face, but she said nothing.

"Aww, c'mon," I said with a wicked grin. "Don't be shy. Isn't this what you wanted? You and me, alone?" I gestured to the car. "You got anything sexy on that'll match the black leather on these seats?"

"We had a deal," she hissed. "And it didn't include you."

"Well, shit changes, don't it? Now hand over the money."

"Why should I?"

"I dunno, maybe 'cause you got us tangled up in some shit I still don't completely understand? Maybe because you tried to kill us both? Because you broke my boy's nose? Or because I've got a knife and I'm kinda pissed off? Fuck, Kell, pick a reason."

Her green eyes blazed. "You wouldn't."

In a flash, I pinned her to the seat by the throat, my knife centimeters from her left eye.

"Just like you wouldn't shoot me in the cargo bay, right, Kell?" I whispered, leaning close enough to smell her perfume. All the color drained from her already-pale features, and I felt her shudder in my grip.

"Okay, okay," she squeaked. "It's up front. The duffel bag is in the passenger seat up front."

I released her. "Wise move."

I reached over the seat and pulled up a blue duffel bag, which I pulled to the back with us and tossed to Kell.

"Open it."

"Why do you—"

"Open it."

She unzipped the bag, revealing banded stacks of UNF deposit bills. A quick look at the holograms and glowing crypto keys told me they were real. She moved the bills around to show me there was nothing else in the bag.

"That's enough. Now close it."

She zipped it closed and stared at me.

"I was serious, in the letter," she said. "I didn't mean for it to wind up like this, and I really did get to like him."

"Like him? You tried to kill him."

"No, I tried to kill you. It was panic when I pointed the gun at him. Besides, all that was just business."

"That makes no fucking sense."

"It's complicated."

"Yeah, I see that."

"Tell him—"

"I ain't telling him shit from you, Kell. Go fuck yourself."

With that, I opened my door and sprinted down the alleyway, Kell's shouted curses pushing me even faster.

———————

Ten minutes later, Carla's rented truck screeched to a halt outside our Black Sun 490's open cargo bay.

"C'mon, Carla," I said.

She shook her head. "Kell knows where the ship is, and she may have been waiting to come before because she didn't think she had a big enough crew. Now that you've fucked her out of the deal, she's gonna be desperate. She'll be here soon enough, which means you shouldn't be."

"Aww, c'mon, it won't take that long."

"You are not doing a very good sales job there, Romeo," she said with a shake of her head. "That's just what every girl wants to hear: 'it won't take that long.' Why do I hang out with you again?"

I shrugged. "I make you laugh or something? Isn't that how that bit usually goes?"

She laughed. "That you do, Snake. And sometimes, you even manage to be good at other stuff too." She gave me a sly grin.

"Next time, then? Where are you and Jade going, anyway?"

"Coltrane, maybe. Not completely sure, but I'll get back up with you soon enough and let you know. And don't worry about me, by the way, even though I know you wouldn't anyway."

"Hey, that's not fair," I protested. "I offered to help. Besides, you're always playing the woman of mystery, so I don't have a clue what you're even up to when I'm not around."

She nodded. "Now you're getting the picture."

"What's that supposed to—"

"Don't worry about it, Snake. Now get outta here before shit goes sideways again. And remind your boss I told him 'never trust a pretty face.' Seriously, you'd think he'd learn by now."

"I'll tell him," I said as I opened the door. "See you around," I shouted over the roar of the Black Sun's engines.

"You too! Later, Snake!" she shouted back. I slammed the door, and the truck pulled away. I bounded up the ramp, bag of cash in hand.

The boss stood at the top, giant grin breaking out when he saw I had the bag in my hand.

"You know what, Snake? I take back one of the terrible things I've said about you."

"Which probably still leaves an infinite number, doesn't it?"

"Yeah, pretty much. Now let's get outta here."

"That's a big fat *roger* on that," I said as I closed the cargo bay door and followed him to the midships. He climbed into his seat, and I dropped down into the turret, depositing the biggest payday we'd ever had on the couch.

We took off, blasting out of the atmosphere at maximum power, and I kept up a good scan to make sure no one followed us off the surface. Radar showed Meridian approaches to be clear, but I didn't breathe easy until the planet was a small brown-and-green marble behind us. I gave it a middle finger from my turret as it grew smaller.

"Okay, so where to now?" I asked.

"We still got one dog to shake," the boss said. "And that means a trip through someplace we know they'll pick up our scent."

I frowned. "Uh, I don't quite get what you're—"

"Schrödinger's cat, remember? Jesus, Snake, do you pay attention at all?"

"Oh, yeah. That. Okay, yeah. I forgot, that's all." I still had no clue what he meant.

"We'll head for the R-122 and make for Macau Station. That ought to do the trick."

"Macau? You sure that's the smartest—"

"Where else you gonna move eighty grand in actual cash, Snake? And it's a hell of a lot closer than New Reno."

"Yeah, but the last time we went to a casino, you blew like ten grand."

"I was up, damn it, until—"

"Until you weren't, boss. Which is kinda how that whole thing works."

"Well, look, it's eighty grand that fell into our laps, okay? So, we'll spend some of it on repairs and maybe a nav system upgrade, but we deserve to have a good time—or at least I do."

"You do? Like I don't? Who was it that brought back eighty grand again? Me or you?"

"Sure, it was you. Of course, the only reason you were the one to do it was because you got outwitted by Michael Ver, shitty singer and even shittier boxer, but who's apparently pretty good at getting away from a dude who prides himself on his street smarts."

"Shut up."

"Like I said, we head for Macau, wash a little bit of this cash, have a good time, and then be on our way."

"If you say so."

"I do."

"Well, as long as I have enough of it to drink the good bourbon and hang out at the craps tables for a few—"

The radar beeped, and I looked down at my screen. Two blips showed, dead ahead and closing fast. The IFF codes were blank.

"I see 'em, Snake," the boss said before I could even speak. "Let 'em get close, we'll have a little conversation, and then we'll be clear."

"But—"

"You really don't understand the plan, do you?" he asked.

I felt my ears going red. "Of course I do, I just—"

"Then shut up and let me handle it."

Within minutes, the two dots on screen had resolved into a Hyundai-Fiat-Chrysler Centurion and an Io Aerospace Lancer. I began to sweat, thinking about what a shame it would be to die without getting a chance to spend that eighty grand.

For his part, the boss seemed unconcerned, not bothering to alter our course even when it was obvious the ships were drifting apart as we got closer, preparing to attack us along different vectors to make my job that much more difficult. I scanned for missile locks, hoping whatever the plan was made more sense than I gave it credit for.

A voice came across the comms. "Black Sun 490, word in the black is you got a little something hot."

"It's not my cargo," the boss said. "I picked it up clean for a client, and I'm being paid to deliver it. If it's hot, take it up with him."

"Now, that ain't the way it works, and you know it," the voice said.

"The bounty doesn't specify a ship registry number, so if you come after me without verification, that's straight piracy, and you know it."

"And you'd be dead right," the voice said. "But the problem with being dead right is that you're still dead. So, dump it now or—"

The boss's radar buzzed in the cockpit at the same time I recognized the waveform of a missile radar on my VDU. "He's got lock!" I shouted as I pressed the countermeasures button and the boss rolled the ship, punching the afterburners as he did so.

Laser fire filled space in front of us as the Centurion opened up. We were still too far for accurate fire, but he managed to score a few hits, and the boss juked us left.

"Is this part of the plan?" I shouted as I tried to set up a shot on the maneuvering Lancer.

"Well, not exactly, but kind of?" he answered as he snap-rolled us away from a long burst of crimson laser fire.

"Okay, I admit it," I said squeezing off a few bolts at the Lancer. "I don't get the plan, so just explain it to me, okay?"

"Not the time, Snake," the boss said over the noise of warning alarms in the cockpit.

The ship shook as my VDU told me our top shields were down to forty-three percent. I swore under my breath and let loose with a long burst that forced the Centurion off his preferred firing position at our six. The boss rolled the ship along its x axis to keep him in my cone of fire and I notched a few hits, dropping his shields to nearly nothing and forcing him to back away.

Meanwhile, the Lancer used this opportunity to stitch us up our port side, scoring enough hits to march our shields below twenty-five percent. He tried to reacquire a missile lock, but I anticipated and countered. He still launched the shot, though, and I watched as it streaked harmlessly below us, exploding in a flash of light three kilometers away.

"All right, all right!" the boss yelled over the comms. "Cease fire and you can have this shit, okay? I'm just doing a run, get it? I'm not trying to get hulled!"

"That's more like it," the voice said. "Dump it and run and we won't follow, but try anything sneaky and I promise you're gonna regret it."

"Dumping," the boss said, and the clang-whoosh from the cargo bay told me he'd expelled the shipping container and probably about twenty-five hundred credits' worth of spare parts into the void. I slewed my turret over to verify and noticed that while the container was indeed gone, most of what went with it seemed to be cardboard and scrap metal, as if the boss had taken the time to secure the spare parts in the bay while I'd been out stealing the money from Kell.

"Now that's the good stuff, right there, merchie. Thanks, and be on your way," the voice said.

"Yeah, roger," the boss said and hit the afterburners.

A flash of light told me the Lancer had fired another missile, and I watched it traverse the distance between the fighter and the shipping container like a bolt of lightning. The container vanished in a blast of fragments, streaking orange in a million directions.

I had a sudden moment of clarity.

"Okay, so I get it now," I said. "We dump the container, which is what the bounty is on, and they just blew the fuck out of it, so that means we're clear, even if Ver isn't inside, because they won't realize that until he shows back up again, I guess."

"I'm glad you finally figured it out," the boss said patronizingly. "You get a gold star for today."

"But my question is, who the fuck is Schrödinger? And what the fuck does his cat have to do with anything?"

"You know what? Forget what I said about the gold star, Snake. You just lost it."

"Fuck you and your gold stars, man."

CHAPTER TWENTY-ONE

A week and a half later, we were three days into our stay at the Golden Phoenix Palace on Macau Station, and life was looking up. We'd spent about twenty thousand credits on an upgrade to the ship's navigation system, better capacitors for the guns, and a total rebuild for engine three. Surprising us both, we'd also managed to get up almost fifteen grand at the tables, which is how the boss and I found ourselves in the high roller craps room, me drinking top-shelf bourbon and him sipping on a nice eighteen-year scotch.

"You know, there's only one thing wrong with this whole picture," he said as we smoked cigars and looked through the room's completely transparent glass floor at the whales swimming in the massive aquarium beneath us.

"And what is that?" I asked, taking another sip of bourbon.

"Now, you're gonna say this is crazy, but I miss Kell," he said.

"Nope, I'm not gonna say that's crazy, boss. I'm gonna say that is batshit insane. Besides, I seem to remember you saying you weren't ever even gonna think about her again."

He shrugged. "Yeah, but I'd still like to know how much of it was real and how much of it was just to try to keep control of Ver."

"Well, she told me that she never wanted it to turn out the way it did, so take that for what it's worth, I guess."

"When did she say that? You never told me that!"

"I just did, didn't I?"

"No, seriously, Snake, when did she say that?"

"Well, I mean, she kind of alluded to it when I took the money, but I figured she'd already told you that when you two had your meeting."

"We didn't have much of a meeting, really," the boss said, frowning into his scotch. "She tried to say something about 'you and me' or whatever, but I wasn't having it and told her she had two hours to come up with the cash or else I was gonna sell Ver off to the other side."

"Ah."

"Yeah. I guess maybe it isn't Kell I miss so much as that I'd just like to get the real story, you know? Least she could've done was leave me a note or some shit."

I took another swallow of bourbon. "Uh-huh."

His eyes narrowed.

"*Snake.*"

"What?"

"Don't fucking 'what' me, motherfucker. You're hiding something."

"Bullshit."

"Nope, not bullshit. The way you said 'uh-huh' was what was bullshit. What do you know that I don't?"

"You mean in general?" I asked. "'Cause we don't have that much time."

"You know what I mean."

I sighed. "Fine. So, she, uh, did leave a note, actually. I found it that night before you two went off and then came back and she tried to shoot me."

"What? And you never told me?"

"I asked you! You said you didn't want to read anything she'd written or ever see her again," I protested. "You said that, not me! Don't try to pin shit on me this time. I asked. You answered. Boom—end of story."

"Do you still have it? Did you read it?" He paused. "I don't even know why I'm asking you that. Of course you fucking read it, didn't you?"

"Maybe I did, yeah. So? How was I supposed to know it was meant for you until I read it to figure out what it was?"

"I dunno, Snake. Did it have my name on it?"

"Maybe, yeah."

"Well, hand it over then."

"I can't. I threw it away when we landed here and cleaned out the ship." I held up my hand to prevent what I knew was coming next. "And don't even start whining. Like I said before, I'd already asked and you said you didn't want to read it, so I—"

"You didn't tell me she'd actually written one! I thought it was a hypothetical!" he shouted.

"Well, you thought wrong."

He finished his scotch and glared at me as he took a long drag from his cigar.

Finally, he spoke. "Okay, since you decided to read it, tell me what she said. All of it."

"Christ, man, I don't remember all of it. It was something like 'I'm really sorry it all worked out like this, but I didn't mean to hurt you and it's for the best, blah blah blah. Love, Kell.'"

"You know what, Snake? You're the worst. Like, really the absolute worst."

"Whatever. I don't even feel guilty about this one, bossman. Like I said, the way you talked, I didn't figure you ever wanted to have anything to do with her again, so I didn't bother keeping it."

A waiter walked up, wearing the type of faux-sad smile people have when they're coming to tell you something their job makes them pretend to be unhappy about. "I'm sorry, gentlemen, but this room is closing in preparation for a private party. Please take your belongings and head to the Xavier Room if you'd like to continue to play craps or the Bolivar Room if you'd prefer to switch to high-stakes poker."

I nodded and stood, grabbing the heavy duffel bag of cash and chips beside me. The boss rose as well, still frowning.

"Look, boss, I know how to make it up to you," I said. "If you'll let me drop this fucking bag off at the vault like I've been telling you we should, we can go out to the Raven Club on C deck, okay? Even I know it's the priciest club in the sector, and the only way you get in is either be straight up smokin' hot or get comped tickets like we did. I guarantee you'll find somebody to take your mind off Kell over there."

"I dunno," he said as we walked down the marble staircase toward the upper floor main lobby and elevators.

"Whaddya mean you don't know?" I asked. "Everybody here is here for a good time! The girls over there are looking for the same good time you are. C'mon, man."

"I didn't mean 'I dunno' about the Raven Club. I meant I dunno about depositing the money at the safe. It's safer with us."

I squinted at him. "How the fuck do you figure that? This place is a casino, boss! A big part of what they do is store money—nobody's gonna fucking take our sack of cash when there's a fucking trillion credits or whatever next to it in the vault! I'm sick of having to babysit this thing anyway, and I'm paranoid we're gonna get too drunk and leave it at a table or something. I wake up like five times a night to check and make sure it's still in my room. It's driving me crazy. Just let me take it down and leave it in the very capable hands of the private army they call security around here, and let's go have a good time."

He shook his head. "I still don't like it, Snake."

"Oh, come the fuck on," I said, rolling my eyes.

"I'm just not—"

I ignored him and strode across the acre of fine carpeting in front of us to a massive set of gold-and-red leather doors emblazoned with *The Peacock Room*. He followed me through the doors and into a dark, ornate lounge lit by cool blue and pink neon, where every table seemed to be occupied by beautiful people drinking stupidly complicated cocktails. I scanned the dim room until I saw a high-topped table with a pair of pretty brunette thirty-somethings in sleek, strappy dresses that looked complicated as hell to put on but probably pretty easy to take off.

"Snake, where are you—"

I marched right up to the table and flashed them a winning smile. "Hey ladies, I'd love to hit on you, but unfortunately I've got this big bag of money, see?" I opened the duffel bag to reveal our cash and chips. "And I've got to take it all down to the vault, but my buddy here's a bit sad and I don't want to leave him alone, because his last girl tried to kill us before she left him."

The boss went red, but the brunette on the left's eyebrows went up. "That's your approach strategy? Are you serious?"

"Completely," I told her. "No bullshit. But get this, my boy here knew she was a scheming bitch and took the bullets out of his pistol, just like you see on the holos, so when she pulled it on us and tried to stamp me, well… I'm still here talking, right?" I grinned and spread my arms. "So, listen, if you two could just cheer him up, that'd be great. All our drinks get comped here anyway, so he's buying, and when I get back, we've got tickets to Club Raven if you two are interested."

They looked at each other. "I think you're probably full of shit," the one on the right said with a smile. "But in a good way."

I smiled back. "I try."

"So why hasn't your friend said anything?" the girl on the left asked.

"I already told you. He's sad."

"Yeah, I'm sad all right," the boss said. "Because everywhere I go, I go with this showboating asshole."

They laughed.

"One more thing before I go," I said. "Do you two like Michael Ver?"

The girl on the left shook her head. "He's cute, but he seems like a bit of a douche."

"And his music kinda sucks," her friend added.

"That is *excellent*," I said. "Absolutely *outstanding*, because may I present to you, appearing for one night only—well, okay, so maybe 'one night only' is bullshit—the very guy who knocked Michael Ver out on Yeager about two weeks ago." I made a melodramatic bow and indicated the boss.

"Bullshit," the girl on the right said.

"Nope, he's serious," the boss said, smiling as he took a seat across from them. "Look it up."

"No fucking way," she said, but her friend pulled out her phone.

"No fucking *way*," she said again as they watched the video and looked across the table at my smiling boss.

I left the boss a handful of high-dollar chips should he need them, and made my way out of the Peacock Room and to the elevators. I pressed the button marked *Vault Level*, and a muscular casino security guard slid in just as the doors closed. He smiled politely at me and nodded as he scanned his badge on the reader and pressed the button marked B3.

I didn't think much of it until I realized the elevator didn't stop at the vault and kept descending, headed toward B3, two levels below.

"That's kind of inconvenient," I told him. "You'd think the elevators would stop on the vault level even though you've got a priority card."

"Yeah, the system is kind of weird that way," he said.

The doors opened on B3 with a ding. He gave me the same polite smile he'd given me before.

Then he punched me in the stomach.

CHAPTER TWENTY-TWO

I collapsed to my knees and got a hard kick in the ribs that sent me to the floor.

He dragged me out of the elevator, but I had the good sense to keep ahold of my bag, so it didn't go back up when the doors closed.

He kicked me again, lifted me off the ground like a rag doll, and tossed me through an unmarked door into a windowless room lit by a single fluorescent light bulb. I stood, instinctively reaching for my knife that wasn't there, and got a punch in the face for my trouble, followed by the security guard grabbing me in a full nelson and pressing my face into the wall.

The door opened again, and the security guard spun me around to face a beefy Asian man in an expensive suit with a wide, insincere smile on his face.

"I don't know what's going—" I managed to get out before he slugged me in the face.

"You don't know me, do you?" he asked.

"N-no, I d-don't think so," I said, trying to count my teeth with my tongue.

He punched me in the gut, knocking the wind out of me, and followed it up with an open palm strike to the side of my head that left my ears ringing. I tried to wiggle away, but the security guard's grip never wavered and all I got for my effort was him increasing the pressure, threatening to pull my shoulders out of their sockets.

The Asian man kneed me in the groin, and I felt tears in my eyes.

I moaned. "What the fuck do you want? I don't even know what's going on."

"I am Jason Wu."

The name meant nothing to me, but I didn't have a whole lot of time to really think about it much, because he hit me with a body blow that I was pretty sure cracked a rib. He smacked me across the face again and lifted my chin so he could see me.

"Well?" he asked.

"I-I-I d-don't know any Jason Wu's," I slurred.

His smile spread wider. "Of course, you don't," he said. "And yet, you ordered breakfast using my name on Yaeger two weeks ago. Even though you don't know me. Very rude, wouldn't you say?"

He hit me in the stomach again, and the security guard dropped me into a heap on the floor.

Breakfast? I thought as best I could through the pain until I remembered my little trick at The Grand Star on Yaeger.

Oh.

This guy was *that* Jason Wu? I mean, I understood getting angry, but this seemed a bit much for a fucking breakfast.

I coughed, and a searing pain shot through my ribs.

"I'm really sorry," I rasped. "Really, really, really sorry about the breakfast—like, you have no idea how sorry I am right now. But, uh, don't you think—"

"Don't I think it's too much? Of course, it is. But I am a man who lives in a casino. Everything is too much."

"Like I said," I moaned, "I'm sorry, and—"

He kicked me and I curled into the fetal position, closing my eyes against the pain.

"But to be honest," he continued, "I never even would have gotten the chance for revenge had I not been discussing my peculiar complaint with a very good friend of mine, who also has an interest in you, it seems."

The door opened and closed again, and when I opened my eyes, I saw a pair of tall, shiny red heels. I winced as I followed a long, pale set of legs up to a tight green skirt and white silk shirt.

Kell smiled down at me.

"Hello, Snake. Surprised to see me?"

I tried to answer but could only manage a whimper.

"That's right, Snake, it was an interesting coincidence that led us here. Mr. Wu and I were on the *City of Joy* coming back here when we got to discussing our mutual bad luck during recent trips to Yaeger. He mentioned that somebody had pulled a fast one on him by getting his name and room number and then charging an expensive breakfast to his account, and I thought to myself—well, I know somebody who that sounds just like. When he showed me the surveillance footage from the hotel, I couldn't have been happier, since I'd already tracked you two here. Given Mr. Wu's great importance to the station, with his help, this has all been much easier."

"W-what do you want from me, Kell?" I mumbled. "I don't have Ver anymore."

She chuckled. "I know that, Snake. Ver came back to pick up filming again four days ago. I didn't come for Ver. I came to get my money back."

"Your money?"

"Yes, my money. You know that cash you've got in that duffel bag? I'm in the insurance business, Snake. We don't pay out unless we absolutely have to, and we don't pay out for fraud. And since you didn't uphold your end of the deal? That's fraud, plain and simple."

"You kidnapped your own client!"

"Just business. We insure his life, and his life was never in any danger until you two fucked around and messed things up, and the word got out from Liz's contacts underground that he'd been kidnapped. That's what put all the bounties out trying to settle all of Ver's stupid debts. All we needed was for the shoot to be delayed."

"I-I-I don't understand."

"Of course you don't, because you're not very bright, but I'll explain it to you because when you do get it, it's going to hurt that much worse." She nodded to the security guard behind me, who kicked me again.

"Our competitors insured the shoot," Kell said, kneeling down to talk to me. "For sixteen and a half million credits. If the shoot was delayed more than a week but Ver wasn't dead or hadn't quit the shoot, they paid up. Now, due to some strategic moves by my company in the past year or so, we happened to know this would likely push them out of business. So, all we needed was for Ver to disappear for a week—which is where Liz came in. When you two showed up and punched Ver, it just made things that much easier."

The security guard kicked me again, sending a spasm of pain through my ribcage so intense that I threw up. Kell only just managed to get out of the way. Unfortunately, even the pain couldn't prevent the realization slowly working its way across my brain from arriving.

I closed my eyes and felt even worse, if it were possible.

"But, if V-Ver, came back f-four days ago, then that means y-you…"

She laughed again. "Yes, Snake. That means I won. I won, and our competitor is filing for bankruptcy protection. And that is what I wanted you to know—that in the end, I won."

I watched her as she left the room, stooping to pick up the duffel bag as she did. She turned around in the doorframe and gave me the cheerful smile I'd come to hate.

"Tell your boss I'll see him around," she said.

I groaned.

———————————·

Several hours later, a knock sounded on my door, echoing in my head like gunshots in an empty room.

"Give me a minute," I rasped, and managed to pull myself out of bed and over to the door, which I unlocked and opened.

The boss stood outside, eyes bright and wearing a huge smile, which disappeared when he saw me.

"Oh, shit. What the fuck happened to you?"

"Kell."

"She's here?"

I nodded and retreated back into my room, collapsing onto the bed. He followed me, closing the door and locking it behind him.

"Yeah," I said. "She's here. Or she was. I think she got what she wanted."

"Which was?" he said in a voice that told me he already knew the answer to his question.

"Yeah, she got the money back."

"I told you I didn't want to take it to the vault!"

I waved a hand at him. "She had plenty of help. From inside the casino. She'd have gotten it whether or not I went to the vault. But that wasn't all. She also told me she won. Ver was gone long enough that her company put the competition out of business or something."

"How would that even work?" he asked.

"Look at me, man. Do you think they let me take fucking notes? I'm lucky I'm not dead."

He plopped down into one of the room's ornate leather chairs. "Fuck. *Fuckfuckfuckfuckfuckfuckfuck-fuuuuuuuuuck.*"

"Yeah."

"Well, shit. My night is ruined," he said. "And here I was just coming up so I could take a shower and change before I went out with Emily and Mallory, and figured I'd see if you were in your room. Fuck, I shoulda just not bothered."

"So go take a shower then," I said.

"What? You just lost all the money!"

"Doesn't matter. Our name's still on the Raven Club guest list, and I'm sure you've still got some chips left. May as well enjoy what we got left while you can."

"What about you?" he asked.

"I dunno if you noticed, boss, but I'm not really in dancing shape at the moment. I think I'm just gonna lay here and treat the pain with alcohol."

"We can't stay here," he said. "She knows where we are. We gotta move hotels at least."

"I don't think she's gonna do anything else to us, boss. She coulda killed me down there if she wanted to. And at this point, if she does want to, that's fine by me, because I'd rather die than move anymore right now."

"Man, I dunno about not changing hotels," he said. "What if—"

"You can do whatever you want to, but I'm staying here."

He stood. "Fine, we'll stay, but don't go anywhere. I'll check on you when I get back."

"Motherfucker, do I look like I'm going anywhere except to sleep?"

He rolled his eyes at me and got up to leave.

"Oh, yeah, boss. One more thing."

"What's that?"

"Tell the girls I died and it was my last wish for you to go out with them or something. Even a no-game-having son of a bitch like you should be able to get laid with that setup."

He glared at me as he stood. "How is it, Snake, that even when you deserve sympathy the most, you still don't deserve it at all?"

"It's a talent, really."

DAVID DIXON

Snake and the Boss
will return in...

HELL HAS
NO FURY

HELL HATH NO FURY TEASER

I've seen a lot of shit.

I was on Titan when the Tigers pulled off the Khalil Attack. I flew with Blackie Crisk for six months. I was a block boss in the Greens when we fought the Reds in the Skyla Sector Gang War and wound up aboard the *Braxton* in the securemax unit for my trouble. I've been in God knows how many fistfights, knifefights, and firefights—and cleaned up after God knows how many more. Between gunbattles, decompression accidents, and jailhouse riots, I thought I'd seen the worst humanity had to offer.

But I was wrong.

The boss and I had just landed on Bohr Station and spent six hours arguing with what I thought at the time

was the single dumbest customs officer in the galaxy —
and that's a high bar.

"Jesus H. Christ, what was that?" the boss asked
me when we emerged from the customs office. "You'd
think that dude had never even seen a customs
declaration. How the hell did he make general
inspector?"

"Right there with you, man," I answered.
"'There were discrepancies' he said. We filed an empty
bay, scanned empty, and then landed at tare weight!
What the fuck kind of discrepancy can there be?"

The boss shrugged. "I dunno and to be honest, I
don't care. All I wanna do is get that O2 sensor
replaced and see if that offer we got to haul out to
Basmallah III still stands."

"While you're doing that, I'm going to get up
with Mo and see if I can score a copy of CryptoKiller
that actually works this time," I told him as we
boarded a public tram to docking bay Z where our ship
was parked.

The boss snorted. "What are you going back to
him for? He ripped us for a hundred-fifty credits the
last time we were here for the copy we *do* have. That
software sucks."

"Well, when you're buying pirated shit, it's hard
to complain to the manufacturer, you know? And
when it sells legit for like twenty-five times what you

pay for it, it's hard to complain to the guy you bought a bootleg copy off of either."

The boss frowned. "I guess. But still, money is money. Get us a good deal and try not get ripped off too bad. Again."

"C'mon man, it's me you're talking about here."

"Yeah, I know. That's why I said it."

We kept on bullshitting through our tram ride and all the way through bay Z. Right up until we realized that we'd walked literally *all the way* through the docking bay—that is, we'd walked past all 60 docking stalls and never seen our ship. The massive doors that marked the transition from docking bay Z to ZA loomed in front of us.

"What the fuck?" the boss asked.

"We were in 41Z," I said. "I remember. I swear it's 41Z."

He pulled out the receipt, which we'd never had to do before because it isn't hard to remember where you've parked the only thing you own, especially when it's a cross between your home, your job, and your crazy ex-girlfriend. Forgetting where you docked your ship is like forgetting where you left your dick—it just doesn't happen.

"It's 41Z all right."

We turned around and marched back to 41Z, where we'd parked our spaceworn Black Sun 490 between an Indus 45L and a blue Shoushen of indiscriminate model. The other two small cargo haulers were still there, but our Black Sun was gone—the painted yellow square on the deck that marked our slice of real estate on the station was empty.

We walked to the center of the bay and slowly circled our way around it like absolute idiots, as if the ship could somehow be hiding in a giant open space. The boss even craned his neck to look up, just to be sure it hadn't somehow docked itself on the ceiling, although for all I knew he was looking for a camera to see if someone who had a strange desire to meet a very violent end was fucking with us.

We were so confused that we missed six uniformed Bohr security cops when they showed up from whatever hole cops crawl out of.

"Is there a problem? You two looking for something?" one of the cops asked in a voice soaked in sarcasm. I looked up and was about to let him have a smart remark but noticed that he wasn't alone like the bay guards usually were. He was rolling with a crew. My gut tightened.

The boss seemed to have no compunction about smarting off, though. Either that, or he was too stupid to realize that this was more than just general stop-and-harass cop dickishness.

"Yeah, dipshit. I am looking for something. Two things, actually."

"Which are?" the cop asked.

"Well, first, I'm looking for my ship. You know, that thing you guys are supposed to be guarding while it's parked here?"

"Haven't seen it. Sorry, can't help. But maybe we could make it up to you and help with that second thing you needed," one of the cops said with a wicked grin.

The boss nodded. "Yeah, maybe so. See, I'm looking for your mom's number. She gave it to me when I climbed off her last night, but I seem to have lost it. So if you find it, let me know, okay?"

The cop took it better than I expected, flashing an easygoing smile that his eyes betrayed as false. "Watch it. You really have no idea why I'm here."

It was my turn. "Not exactly, but let me take a few guesses: a C average? Unresolved issues from adolescence? Tiny dick? Never knew your real dad? I dunno, man, you tell us."

I had the bad feeling that this cop was going to give us a hard time no matter what, so I wanted to get in my smart-ass comments while I still had teeth.

"All right, all right," he said, still smiling. "Open mic night is over. You two can come with me the easy way or you can come with me the hard way." His squad took this as a signal to spread out in a loose circle around us.

"Whoa, whoa, whoa," the boss said, raising his hands in front of him to show he wasn't reaching for the revolver I knew was tucked into his shoulder holster. "Let's be cool about this. Since you obviously know what happened to the ship, why don't you just tell us what's going on down here and nobody has to go anywhere."

"Okay, *that's* a lot better. Finally using some sense," the cop said with a nod as he took a step closer to the boss.

I was only able to get out a garbled warning before the cop moved like a striking viper and zapped the boss right in the gut with his stun gun. He crumpled to the ground with a whimper.

The cop looked down at his handiwork, then turned to me with wolfish grin as his goon squad took up positions behind me. I didn't see a way that my combat knife was going to get me out of this one, so I took the only prudent course a man nicknamed Snake could:

"So I guess I'm just gonna wherever you guys say then, all right?"

The cop's smile was real this time. "Yep," he said—right before his buddy got me with a stun gun in the lower back.

I stifled a cry but went to the deck all the same.

The cop squatted down beside me. "Your shit may play with the local yokels, but you have no clue who you're dealing with, so from here on out, you might want to keep the funny comments to a minimum." To make his point, he zapped me with the stun gun again, right in the neck. Zip cuffs slipped over my wrists and one of the goons pulled them tight enough to cut off the circulation.

A windowless, autopiloted work van arrived, holographic police markings already fading to flat black, and the boss and I were unceremoniously hefted up and tossed inside. The rest of the cops, or whoever they were, climbed in after us. None of them said a word as the van accelerated, taking us God-knows-where.

The van slowed to a stop about a half an hour later. I risked a look at our captors, and they rewarded me with another taste of the stun gun. The jolt made me bite my tongue. I tasted blood.

"I fuckin' hate cops," I muttered.

That got me zapped again.

One of them threw a black hood over my head just before I heard the door slide open. Between the darkness, the blood in my mouth and pretty much all my muscles screaming in agony after the stun gun, I wasn't exactly focused on what was around me, but I was still able to make out the boss getting the same treatment. I heard a brief struggle, which I assumed was him wrestling to try to prevent them from getting his pistol, but I knew better than to resist when I felt one of them draw my knife from its scabbard at my back.

They frog marched us up a few sets of steep stairs, down hallways made of metal grating, and through what I guessed was a doorway into a quiet room. Plush carpet felt strange underfoot as I heard a hatch close and a muffled conversation I couldn't make out. A blade sliced my cuffs off, and hand in my chest sent me stumbling backwards. I had a brief moment of panic they'd pushed me off something high before I landed in a soft, supple chair.

The hood came off and the boss and I found ourselves face to face with our antagonist.

He sat across from us, lower half and hands hidden behind a hefty desk. We gaped at him, open-mouthed, for an what had to have been an uncomfortably long time.

The man had skin so pale it was almost transparent, pulled so tight as to make him look less like a man and more like a living corpse—his whole body was the kind of white usually associated with scar tissue. The veins in his head and neck spiderwebbed visibly, and the least movement of his facial muscles was visible through his pallid skin. Adding to the general freakishness of his appearance was the complete lack of hair—not an eyebrow, not a single bit of stubble, and a dome so bald it made me wonder if he'd ever had any hair on his head at all. His eyes were a cold ice-water blue, but less water to drink and more the kind of ice water that awaited passengers on doomed ocean liners. When they flicked from the boss to me without blinking, my skin crawled and I realized that they must be synthetic ocular implants, although they were admittedly the best I'd ever seen.

He flashed a rictus smile and opened his pale lips to reveal gleaming white teeth.

"Well, gentlemen, I trust you're over the unfortunate shock most people have when they meet me in the flesh. There is an explanation behind all of this, which you may yet get to hear—an explanation that most never get the chance to know." He spoke perfect inner-worlds Common, and his diction was as clean and accentless as a computer's. His delivery did nothing to calm my brain which was screaming something along the lines of *run like holy fucking hell*. I risked a glance at the boss who had a look on his face that I'm pretty sure mirrored mine: totally false bravado attempting unsuccessfully to hide our sheer, uncomprehending terror.

"But that does not matter," the pale man continued, "I did not bring you here for conversation, nor to try to move uncivilized men like you two with the pathos of my story. No, I brought you here so that I could talk to you in the most animal of languages—the language of fear."

"*Fear?*" the boss whispered.

"Yes. Fear." The man gave a smile that made me think of every serial killer in every horror holo I'd ever seen. "In ancient times, wise men used to say 'fear of the Lord is the beginning of good works.' It is much the same even now, except *now*, your good works will be inspired by a being much more tangible, intractable, and unmerciful than the deities of old—me."

My head spun. "Uh, I think you've got the wrong—"

"You do not *think*," he snapped. "You *fear*. The problem is, your fear is only the kind of surface fear, the type of unconscious unease that an animal might feel when faced with an unfamiliar predator, but this is not the fear I seek. This is not enough—not for you two."

I had no idea where this guy was going with his soliloquy, but I had a bad feeling that he was right and that I really didn't understand fear yet—and horrifying thought that I soon would.

He continued. "No, I need a conscious fear from the both of you—not the panic of a frightened animal, but the true, deep-seated terror of the annihilation of your existence in every sense of the word."

What the ever-loving *fuck*?

He sighed. "When I set about thinking of how to get you to do what I want you to do, I tried to place myself in your situation, tried to reason out a motive to compel you do what I ask. But I could reason nothing. So then, if not reason—fear. But fear of what?"

"I don't think this is really necessary to—" the boss said.

The man continued, unbothered by the interruption. "It could hardly be fear of danger. You two have faced and escaped death many times before so much so that you cannot truly comprehend what it would mean not to exist. In your line of work, life is short and death quick and cheap, and so therefore life is cheap. Your lives are not valuable enough—even to you—to make you fear losing them."

I didn't like the sound of that at all. I took a quick glance around the plush stateroom, trying to see if I could make a break for it, but the goon squad had the doors covered.

The man's eye's narrowed as he continued, speaking more to himself than to us. "Perhaps pain? I could inflict pain quite literally beyond what you can imagine, but this very failure of your imagination works against me. How can a man fear what he cannot even fathom?" I wasn't sure he was giving me enough credit, really, because I could imagine some pretty painful things. "No. Pain is not the correct tool. But I know what is, because I know the very hope of your existence, which, in your cases, unfortunately manifests itself in a very tangible object."

He let whatever it was hang out there in silence for a moment.

"Your ship," he finished. "It is your ship that makes you different from everyone else, from all the landlubbing 'worms' you flight jockeys despise and look down on. It is your ship that allows you free yourself from the mundane responsibilities of putting down roots, that allows to to reinvent yourselves and remake your image in every little minor planet and system from Earth to the farthest reaches of unfederated space. Without your ship, you are another planetbound dreamer without hope of escape. Just another slave unable to escape his master, another cog in a giant uncaring machine, another speck of dust not at all dissimilar from the millions of other specs of dust on whatever worthless rock he inhabits."

The boss's mouth moved but nothing came out.

"Plato says that a man who has never seen the light cannot appreciate the darkness—and there is the great thing about your fear—that you have seen the light. You know what it is like to live by your own rules, to leave a life behind and make it anew. You can truly *fear* the darkness, because you know the light. There is an old saying that a 'captain is god of his ship.' You two have been gods—small gods, but gods nonetheless—but I can make you mortal."

I started to feel a little defensive, seeing as how I was a hell of a lot more afraid of being killed than losing our piece-of-shit Black Sun 490, and this asshole seemed to be telling me that somehow made me unsophisticated. That said, the look of horror on the boss's told me that while the pale man may have gotten me wrong, he'd gotten him right.

I figured I'd try to see if the creepy motherfucker across from us actually wanted anything from us, or he just got his rocks off scaring the shit out of people before he turned their skins into coats or whatever. "Okay, okay," I said as bravely as I could. "You want us afraid that you're gonna fuck us up in ways we can't even imagine—check. So what exactly do you want from us?"

He picked up a tablet off his desk and turned it to us. Onscreen were our UNF master files—crosslinked to every legitimate computer network in UNF space and accessed as the files of record by even non-federated computer systems. I knew that the master files existed, but as far as I had ever heard, there was no actual way to access the master file, only to make data calls to certain sections. Whatever database he was accessing was obviously way deeper shit than the boss and I were usually into. Below our two files was a copy of the ship's title, each one marked "pending permanent removal."

"Removal of your records from the UNF database will remove from you from every aspect of society. No trace of you will remain. Your ship, which is already impounded, will go up for auction—of course, you will be unable to bid on it, because you could not access your money nor could you have it titled to you, since you do not exist. You will have no licenses, no qualifications—not even an ID number. Even in the underworld you will have reason to fear—how can authorities investigate the disappearance of someone who never existed to begin with?"

Our tormentor sighed and leaned back, ever so slightly, in his chair. "But I offer the opportunity to spare yourselves this fate."

There was a moment of silence.

I *still* wasn't sure what it was he wanted from us. I shivered at the thought that perhaps he'd mistaken us for someone else, then reality kicked in and I realized that someone this meticulous—even if unhinged— probably didn't make a whole lot of mistakes. I was still trying to work out whether that should be encouraging or terrifying when the boss piped up with a bit of his trademark defiance, as futile as it usually was.

"Bullshit. Nobody can just delete somebody out of the UNF database. I don't care what kind of hacker you think you are, it can't be done—the protocols are bulletproof. People have been trying to hack in forever. It can't be done."

This wasn't the best time for me point out the critical flaw in his logic, but I didn't have to. The pale man did it for me, a ghoulish smile playing across his pale lips. "You're right. The system is impregnable, as everyone knows. This is the fundamental truism that underlies all modern commerce. Of course, I cannot hack *in*. Fortunately, this is unnecessary in my case, because *I am already inside*."

"But nobody has access to the—" the boss began.

"As Section Six, I have all the access I require to do what I have already done. Surely even you understand that there is no reason to break into a vault when one stands inside it already?"

My head swam. Section Six? I had trouble breathing.

Section Six?

Section Six didn't even exist! It was a catch all, a made-up, section of the UNF security apparatus. At most, it was a cover story for the activities of the Security Council's black-ops service, Section Five. Everybody—I mean everybody not wearing a tinfoil hat and carrying on about aliens—knew there was no Section Six. The document that gave the security directorates their names was only five sections long. Everybody knew that.

But there had always been whispers.

The Monks of Gethil were supposedly a Section Six operation gone wrong—or depending on who you talked to, gone right. Crazies I'd met in my younger years blamed the Xiamin terraforming disaster on

Section Six. I knew an otherwise sensible guy who swore up and down that Section Six destabilized the palladium market and caused the dissolution of the Indira Republic just before they joined the UNF—even after the scandal of how it happened became public knowledge and brought down the Pasco Secretariat. Section Six—if you believed the loony all-caps posters lurking on the bottoms of message boards who took great lengths to hide their identity—was an unstoppable, all-seeing, all-knowing force of nature so powerful not even the Secretary General could stop them, if he was even cleared to know they existed. They were the fucking invisible boogeyman of UNF space and was no more real than Santa Claus, or the Easter Bunny, or the Galileo Nebula Being.

And yet.

And yet I was sitting across a desk from someone who looked like he'd stepped out of a nightmare, and had access to apparently infinite resources he was going to use to fuck us up more thoroughly than killing us ever could, and who was demanding our cooperation in something before he'd even told us what that something was.

I began to reconsider my position on the Galileo Nebula Being.

I swallowed hard and decided to play dumb, which, given the circumstances, wasn't even really playing on my part. "Section Six?" I asked, trying to sound skeptical. "Section Six, huh? I, uh, didn't think they existed."

"And yet, here I sit," he said. "Although you are, strictly speaking, correct. *They* do not exist. *I* am Section Six. There were two of us in the beginning, but the other is..." He shrugged. "...No longer with us. He passed away in the same unfortunate shuttle accident that killed Secretary General Sakasvilli. Tragic, really. Anyway, with his untimely demise, there is no one else with oversight of the Section, so it is up to me to use the broad scope of my powers as I see fit and in a manner that will best benefit the UNF in the long run."

I realized then that with the full weight of the UNF and with no one to prove he existed or cleared to know what he was up to, there was nobody who could stop him.

He gave me a wicked grin. "So you understand, then. There is no escape from my power. You two are unmade, gentlemen, and while I offer damnation with my left hand, I offer salvation with my right."

"We get it," sighed the boss. "We fuckin' get it. So what the hell do you need us for if you've got everything already?"

"Before my partner shuffled off this mortal coil, he restricted certain... things... from me. Earlier, I explained the uniqueness of my position. There are none like me—just as there were, unfortunately, none like my now-deceased colleague. He restricted access to UNF files that I desperately desire." The anger that passed over the man's eerie features was like a violent storm raging across a barren planet, sending shivers down my spine. "There are certain people I wish to bring under my power, persons I very much wish to speak to, and questions I very much wish to have answered. You will bring me one of those people. Or suffer mightily for failing to do so."

"Who?" the boss and I asked almost simultaneously.

"You know her as Carla."

Oh fuck.

About the Author

David Dixon has been writing fiction and non-fiction for over twenty years. A husband, father of two, and Army veteran whose combat days are long behind him, he lives in Northern Virginia where he writes across a variety of genres and topics. He believes that for every person and every place, there's a story, whether it's a comedy, tragedy, or something in between—and it's his hope to write them all.

More From Dark Brew Press and David Dixon

The Damsel by David Dixon

After a hijacking attempt damages their decrepit Black Sun 490 freighter, Snake and his boss are desperate for cash.

Enter Carla, a gorgeous mercenary bad girl with a job offer that seems too good to be true. Unfortunately for him, while Snake is convinced she's stringing them along to their deaths, he's not the one in charge.

The job gets dicey in a hurry, and it doesn't take him long to figure out a fatal blow is coming. He's just not sure if it will come from the pirates that haunt the nav lanes, knife-wielding goons looking for revenge, Carla herself, or the cheap vodka he drinks to stay sane.

If Snake's going to make it out alive, he'll need every bit of his quick wit—and an even quicker trigger finger.

More From Dark Brew Press

Urban Gothic
by Stephen Coghlan

Burned out and drugged up, Alec LeGuerrier spends his days faking it, barely ekeing out an existence while living in a haze of confusion and medicated mellowness. That is, until he stops a gang of nightmarish oddities from killing a strange young woman with indigo eyes.

Dragged into the lands of the dreaming, he must come to terms with his brutal past and his grim imagined future in a land his body knows is real, but his mind refuses to acknowledge.